"I hope you found who you were looking for."

He hesitated. "Yes, I did. See you tomorrow."

As he left the clinic, her words came back to him—
I hope you found who you were looking for.

He knew she'd been talking about the rescue, but for a split second, he thought she'd been talking about relationships. He'd thought he'd found who he was looking for in Jackie, his ex. The couple who'd been voted most likely to marry in high school had indeed married. Only, it hadn't lasted. He'd married her right before shipping out with the army. But once he came home...

Well, things had changed.

He climbed in his car, and as he pulled away, he could have sworn he saw the curtains in the front window twitch. But when he looked again, they were in the same spot they had been. Must have been his imagination. But man, that had been nothing like his interactions with Doc had been.

And he wasn't sure how he felt about that.

Dear Reader,

I hate to admit it, but I'm afraid of heights.
Like really afraid. Climbing a ladder is about as
adventurous as I get, when it comes to that. So when
I had an idea for a hero who climbs mountains
and rescues people from staggering heights, it kind
of played on all of my fears. Especially as I was
researching the techniques used by rock climbers and
Search and Rescue workers.

But I loved Cabe, my hero, so it was all worth it.
And I was able to vicariously live through him
without having to actually…well, look down.

Thank you for joining Cabe and Jessie as they
journey together through the spectacular scenery of
the Sierra Nevada mountain range, and as they learn
to trust both each other and the idea of love. I hope
you love their story as much as I loved writing it.

Love,

Tina Beckett

THE VET, THE PUP
AND THE PARAMEDIC

TINA BECKETT

HARLEQUIN
MEDICAL
ROMANCE

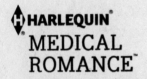

HARLEQUIN®
MEDICAL ROMANCE™

Recycling programs
for this product may
not exist in your area.

ISBN-13: 978-1-335-73756-4

The Vet, the Pup and the Paramedic

Copyright © 2022 by Tina Beckett

Harlequin Enterprises ULC
22 Adelaide St. West, 41st Floor
Toronto, Ontario M5H 4E3, Canada
www.Harlequin.com

Printed in U.S.A.

Three-times Golden Heart® finalist **Tina Beckett** learned to pack her suitcases almost before she learned to read. Born to a military family, she has lived in the United States, Puerto Rico, Portugal and Brazil. In addition to traveling, Tina loves to cuddle with her pug, Alex; spend time with her family and hit the trails on her horse. Learn more about Tina from her website, or "friend" her on Facebook.

Books by Tina Beckett

Harlequin Medical Romance

The Island Clinic collection

How to Win the Surgeon's Heart

New York Bachelor's Club

Consequences of Their New York Night
The Trouble with the Tempting Doc

Risking It All for the Children's Doc
It Started with a Winter Kiss
Starting Over with the Single Dad
Their Reunion to Remember
One Night with the Sicilian Surgeon
From Wedding Guest to Bride?
A Family Made in Paradise

Visit the Author Profile page
at Harlequin.com for more titles.

To my family, as always

CHAPTER ONE

CABE MCBRIDE ONLY shifted his attention for a minute. Just enough time to peer into some of the scrub brush that lined this particular path on the mountain. The narrow, winding way had been treacherous, even though they were still well below the line of snow that clung almost year-round in this part of the Sierra Nevada range. He and Soldier always worked as a team on these rescue missions, his bloodhound's nose an invaluable tool in finding missing persons. And this time was no different. Soldier had alerted him to a scent near this area, which was where Sandra said her husband had last been spotted. And possibly suicidal after losing his job last week.

He turned to see if Soldier was scouring another area, but his dog was nowhere to be seen.

He gave the quick double whistle he used to call his companion back to him. But there was no response. No deep howl to indicate he'd found the missing man. No nothing. There were two other volunteer members of the Sierra Nevada Search and Rescue team also out here, on different ridges. The three college friends were part of the same paramedic squad. There were also two officers out there searching.

He tapped his earbud and spoke into the headset. "Any sign?"

Bradley Sentenna was the first to respond. "Nothing here. Doug, you have anything?"

"Nada." Doug Trapper, who looked like a Grizzly Adams type with his thick beard and longish hair, was a man of few words, but had a huge heart.

"Soldier alerted to something, but I'm having trouble finding him, which isn't like him. Stand by."

"Gotcha."

He switched off his mic and this time called to his dog. "Soldier! Come!"

A faint sound came from the scrub about ten yards to his left. Alarm bells rang in his head. Never had his dog ever failed to respond to him. After rescuing him from a local shelter several years ago, Cabe found his pup had had a natural aptitude for finding things. Including people. So much so that he'd sailed through a rigorous training course with ease. And so began their partnership with the search and rescue team here.

He moved sideways and although the sun was still high in the sky, the shadows cast by the low-lying bushes made it hard to see. Suddenly he spied a shadow crouched in the midst of them. And a pair of shoes. They were as still as…

Hell! He tapped his mic. "Found something. Head this way."

His friends both acknowledged without asking any questions. He pulled in a deep breath and then parted the first set of branches, hoping he was wrong.

"Stay right where you are. I have a gun." The growled words hit him in the midsection. Had he hurt Soldier?

He forced himself to respond calmly, even as his heart pounded in his chest. "Are you injured?"

"No. Not yet. Just don't come any closer. Please."

Not yet?

There was an edge of desperation to the words that made Cabe take another step. He needed to notify law enforcement about the gun, but to do so right now, in front of the man, might bring consequences neither of them wanted. Especially if his wife was right. The psych training he'd had in both the military and as part of his SAR training was telling him she was. So he decided to stall as he assessed the situation. "I'm looking for my dog. Have you seen him?"

There was a pause before the voice came back. "I—I think he went over."

"Over?" Just then he realized what the man meant. There was a steep drop-off just past where the man had hidden himself. Had he heard them coming before he could jump to his death?

The thought of Soldier lying at the bottom of that crevasse broken and bleeding filled his throat with bile.

Stick to the matter at hand, Cabe.

"I think he fell." The man stood. Dressed in a suit and tie, there was no sign of the gun he'd claimed to have. That was a relief. But dirt and sweat were streaked across his face, and his hair looked like a million fingers had tunneled through it. Trying to get up the courage to end it all?

It would be at least twenty or thirty minutes before Doug and Brad made it here. And the officers were also somewhere out there. Probably down at the bottom of the mountain. His medic bag was just to the left of him. Could he make a grab for the man if he turned and tried to leap off the cliff?

Doubtful.

He needed more time. Maybe he could get the guy's mind fixed on something besides his own troubles. Gain some kind of rapport with him.

"Where?"

"Over there. He was coming toward me, and then all of a sudden he seemed to scrabble for his footing and disappeared." The man's eyes met his. "I—I didn't push him. I swear. I would never hurt an animal."

No. Just himself.

Damn, if Soldier really had fallen, he needed to act. But first he needed to make sure of the man's intentions. "Where's the gun."

The other man shook his head, eyes shifting away. "I don't have one. I just wanted to be left alone."

Cabe decided to take him at his word. "I don't know why you came up here, but right now, I need help with my dog. Can you see clear to give me a hand?"

"I guess so."

This was obviously not how the man had expected his day to go. Or to end. And maybe that was a good thing.

"I have some rope and climbing gear behind me. If he's down there, I'll need you to feed the rope through a pulley. Can you do that?"

The man nodded.

Cabe looked at him a little closer. "I take it you're Randolf Meridian?"

Another nod. A little sharper this time. "How do you know who I am?"

"Your wife is really worried about you. She called search and rescue."

"I wish she hadn't. She'd be better off if…"

"Why do you think that?"

He gave a half shrug. "She's smart and successful and her daddy once told me she could do a hell of a lot better than a stockbroker. I'm beginning to think he was right."

Cabe bit off a swear word. "He's not. Your wife loves you."

Hell. He paused, trying to decide whether to impart the next bit of information or not. But the guy needed to know it was not just his wife who would suffer if he did what Cabe thought he was planning to do. "There's more. She was going to tell you today. She's expecting a little one. She baked a cake and everything."

Randolf's eyes closed, and he pressed his fingers to his temples for several long seconds. "God! A—a baby? There's no way I can be a father."

"Yes, you can. That little one deserves to know who you are."

The man shook his head. "Like I said, they'd both be better off without me."

Had he really just said that? A sliver of anger went through him. He had heard those words over and over throughout his childhood. A litany that repeated endlessly. Until one day it really had ended. Forever. "Do you really believe that? Do you really want your child to know that his or her father threw his life away…that they didn't mean enough for him to at least try?"

Realizing his voice had risen slightly, he sucked down a breath. "I think both your wife and baby deserve more than that." He gave him a pointed look. "Don't you?"

Soldier was still down there somewhere. But unless Cabe sorted this out right now, it was doubtful he would get much help out of the man. He might even take off once Cabe had climbed down the steep slope. But if he could turn him into an ally, maybe he could turn this around. And right now he sensed if he tried to radio law enforcement, his chance to do that would probably be nil.

"I guess so. I don't know. I can't think." His palm scrubbed at the back of his neck.

"I know it's all confusing right now. But don't make a decision that you can't take back. That you'll never be able to take back, without at least talking to your wife. I wouldn't be out here on this mountain, if she didn't care. *Really* care. Will you at least think about calling her?"

Randolf gave a defeated nod. "Yes."

Cabe studied him for a moment, before deciding the man was telling the truth. A trickle of relief chased the perspiration down his back. Now to seal the deal.

"Good. There's time to sort all of that out later. But right now, I need your help with my dog. He came up here to help me help you. Can't you do the same for him?"

Randolf's chest heaved, and he nodded. "Yes. I'm pretty sure I know where he landed. I heard a thud to our right."

"That helps. Stay close, okay?" Cabe's gut clenched. How big of a thud?

He peered over the edge but couldn't really see much. "You're sure he went down here."

"Yes. What do you need me to do?"

Grabbing the basic equipment he'd brought, he attached one of his pulleys to a nearby tree, attached the rope through it and then fastened the other end to the D-ring on his climbing vest. "I'm going to climb down and take a look. Just keep tension on the rope and feed it through the pulley. Can you do that?" He wouldn't be able to use his manual ascender for the trip back up, because he'd have his hands full with Soldier.

"Yes."

"I'm counting on you." He kept one eye on Randolf and the other on his gear.

"I know."

Cabe blew out a breath and then backed

up to the edge of the slope, sending a couple of loose rocks skittering down the embankment. A soft whine sounded from below. At least Soldier was alive. For now, anyway.

I'm coming, boy.

He looked at Randolf. "I have a couple of friends who are on their way to help, so just follow my instructions until they get here, okay?"

"Cops?"

"No. But there are a couple of officers at the base of the mountain awaiting word. They're concerned for your safety. Nothing more."

"She really called out the cavalry, didn't she?"

"That should tell you something."

"It does." He looked Cabe in the eye. "She's really having a baby?" Those words seemed firmer, as if he'd come to some kind of decision. Cabe only hoped it was the right one.

"She really is. Feed the rope for me, okay?"

Randolf gave a nod.

With the immediate threat pushed to the side for the moment, Cabe took a deep breath and hoped beyond hope, Soldier wasn't mortally wounded. He slowly put one foot behind the other as he let the rope take some of his weight. Everything held. At least so far. And Randolf was doing just as he instructed, giving him support as he inched his way down the slope.

It seemed to take forever, although it was probably only a period of five minutes before he could see the lower part of the mountain. Then his feet hit a flat area. Rocks went over the side, making an ominous skittering sound as they bounced off whatever was beyond it. Hell. This was little more than a ledge followed by another sharp drop. He doubted there was enough rope to get him all the way down it. If Soldier wasn't here... If he'd struggled...

"Soldier! Where are you boy?"

Another whimper came from just past a patch of scrub. He called up to Randolf. "I'm going to move to your right. Just keep feeding the rope as I move."

"Got it!"

His voice was still firm. Solid. That was a good sign.

Crab-walking sideways, he moved in the direction of the sound. "I'm coming, boy."

Another whimper. At least he was alive. He'd adopted Soldier almost five years ago, just as he was leaving army life behind. As a tribute to all the men he had treated on the field as a medic, he named the dog after them. Brave and loyal, his pup reminded him of the men he had served during his ten years of service.

"Almost there, Soldier." He stepped over another low bush and saw a patch of red fur. Another large step and his dog came into view. The second Soldier saw him, his thick tail thumped on the ground, making Cabe's heart cramp. "I'm here, boy." He crouched beside the dog and immediately saw the problem. He'd fallen on a sharp branch that had impaled the fleshy part of the dog's thigh. He tried to move toward Cabe then fell back with a sharp cry.

"Stay!" He forced his voice to give a sharp warning, not because he was angry, but he didn't want the dog to do more damage to his leg. So he called up. "I found him. Can you give me just a little slack?"

The rope went loose. For a second his heart leaped into his throat, then from above him,

Doug's voice came. "I'm here, Cabe! Let us know what you want."

Thank God.

"Soldier's impaled himself on a pretty big stick. I need to cut it close to the wound and…" He couldn't bring himself to say the rest. Hell. He was as cool as a cucumber with almost every emergency situation he found himself in, but the thought of causing his dog any more pain…

"Got it," Doug called. "Let us know when you're ready."

"Will do. Randolf, I'll need you to give Doug a hand, okay?" He was thankful at least one of his friends had arrived. Both for his and Soldier's sake, but also for Randolf, who had a lot of things on his mind right now.

"I will."

He looked at the area around Soldier. There was some blood, but not enough to indicate that his boy had severed a major vessel. But canine anatomy was not the same as human. He had no choice but to try to free him. The leg that was trapped was the hind one closest to the ground. Taking a pair of sharp cutting pliers from one of the pockets in his vest, he patted Soldier's head. "Easy, boy. We're going to get you out, but it's going to hurt like hell."

Soldier's tail patted the ground as if he understood.

He eased the cutters as close to the dog's wound as he dared. "Stay."

Soldier had been trained to freeze like a statue at that command. But the dog had never sustained an injury like this one either. And he had nothing to cover his eyes or face with. Hell, if he bit him, so be it. But there was no way he was leaving him for one second longer than necessary. The powerful nippers easily cut through the branch, but not without bringing a sharp cry of pain from his dog. Now he somehow had to ease Soldier off the remaining part of the branch. He didn't dare try to reach under him to cut the bottom part.

"This is going to hurt, boy. I'm sorry." He made his hands as flat as possible and slid them under the dog's thigh on either side of the branch. "One, two, three!" Whether he was counting for Soldier's sake or his own, he had no idea, but he lifted the dog's leg up and off the spike of wood, bringing a gut-wrenching howl from his friend.

But he couldn't stop now. He pivoted the dog's body so that he could set the leg back down on top of his own, to avoid contaminating it any more than necessary. Warmth that could only be from blood seeped through his pants, but although he held his breath and waited, the flow didn't pulse in thick streams that would signify an arterial bleed. He exhaled in relief as he did a quick check of the rest of the dog's body, palpating ribs and limbs as best as he could. Nothing broken that he could tell.

He called up to the top. "I have him free. But you guys are going to have to drag us both up, since I don't have a free hand. Can you do it?"

"We're all here now, so between the three of us we have you. Tell us when."

Okay, so Brad was there as well. The only way he figured he could do this was to cradle Soldier on his lap and wrap his own body around the hundred-and-fifteen-pound dog. His rope was geared for two good-sized adults, so it should hold.

Soldier thumped his tail again, lifting his

head to look at Cabe. The threat of moisture made his vision blur for a second before he blinked it away. "Good boy. You're doing great. Another big ouchie coming."

Sliding his left arm under the dog's shoulder, he dragged him the rest of the way onto his lap. This time there was no cry, not even a whimper. Pulling him closer, Cabe drew his knees up and curled his torso over the dog to lock him in place, using his arms to hold him there. Hopefully it would cushion his ride at least a little. He yelled up, "Okay, start pulling."

Since he'd moved sideways to get to Soldier, the first pull of the rope dragged him diagonally across the ground. With each upward heave, his back glanced off rocks and branches tore at his protective clothes. But he didn't ease his grip. It was the least painful way to move his dog, and Cabe would rather take the brunt of whatever they were going over.

Damn! His right shoulder hit something with enough force to make him see stars, but somehow he managed to hold on to Soldier. After ten minutes of effort, hands reached down and hauled them over the side of the embankment.

Brad took one look at him and winced. "Man, you look like hell."

That got a smile out of him. Cabe could have guessed that. His cheek stung from one of the branches that had grabbed at his skin. "That doesn't matter right now."

His eyes searched out Randolf and found him standing beside his two friends, the rope still in his hands.

"How is he?" The man's voice was a bit shaky as he looked back at him.

"He's alive, but I need to get him to a vet. Thanks for helping."

Cabe hadn't moved. In reality, Doug was right. He was beat up. Every muscle in his body ached, and he wasn't sure he could straighten up. At least not easily. He glanced down at Soldier to see liquid brown eyes meet his with a lot more calmness than his own tripping heart.

Brad nodded. "Randolf's going to help us get Soldier down the mountain."

His friend's voice told him, he'd assessed the situation without Cabe needing to fill him in in front of the man. That was good.

And Doug was standing off to the side, his cell phone to his ear. Probably talking to the officers. Or maybe calling Randolf's wife.

Pulling out a square foil pack that Cabe recognized as a reflective survival blanket, Brad shook it out and laid it on the ground just as Doug rejoined them. "I think this will hold under Soldier's weight. We'll put him on it and carry him down the hill like a gurney."

"Yes, that should work."

Uncurling his stiff body, he watched as his two friends and Randolf carefully took Soldier from him and laid him on the blanket. The dog whimpered once and then lay still.

Now came the test when Doug came over and held his hand up. "Can you stand?"

"Yep." He allowed his friend to help him to his feet, his muscles screaming with each movement. It was a small price to pay.

He glanced at Randolf. "Hey, buddy, there are some officers you'll need to talk to. Doug or Brad will help you find them. You have to promise me you'll be honest about your struggles, and that you'll go and talk to your wife."

"Will they arrest me?"

"Like I said, they're more interested in

your well-being. They can help you find someone to talk to. Do it. Not for me. Not for Soldier. Do it for your wife and your new baby. And most of all, for yourself."

"I will. I promise."

Cabe pulled a card out of his pocket. "This is my number. I want you to call me in a couple of days and let me know how it's going. If you don't, I'm going to pay you a visit."

Randolf held up his hands. "I know it was stupid. The shock of losing my job, just as we were in the process of buying a house came up and overwhelmed me."

He understood. All too well. When his father had been at his worst, he'd been overcome by emotions that never should have seen the light of day. At least Randolf didn't seem to have lost himself in a bottle. Which meant he could still think, could still take control of his life. And it sounded like he'd have help doing that, from how scared his wife had sounded. He hoped they would both seek help to get past this.

"I get it. Just don't do anything like that again."

Randolf nodded. "I'd like to help you get him down the hill, if that's okay. And then

I'll talk to the officers. As soon as I call my wife."

"I think that is the best idea I've heard all day."

Jessie leaped up from her little garden, brushing the dirt from her hands as soon as she set down the phone. Her first emergency case as the new vet in the area. And it had to be on a Saturday when her only employee was out of town on a fishing trip. She reached in her pocket for the key to the medical cabinet in her office and squeezed it tight. A habit from her last several weeks in San Francisco. She forced her fingers to uncurl.

Well, she wasn't in San Francisco any longer, and from what old Doc Humphrey had told her last week as he was retiring, the Santa Medina Veterinary Clinic sometimes saw pets who were injured while exploring the wild surrounds of the area. Only this time it wasn't a tourist's pet, it was a search and rescue dog who'd evidently fallen down a steep embankment and been injured during a rescue.

Fortunately Doc Humphrey had bequeathed her the small cottage that was on the clinic's property, where he'd lived. He was moving to Idaho where his daughter was, wanting to make the most of his time after getting a diagnosis for the slight palsy he'd developed. Parkinson's. It was still in its early stages, but her heart hurt at the pain in his eyes when he realized he'd have to give up his practice here. He'd been in a hurry to find a replacement, and she'd been in a hurry to relocate out of the city.

Not bothering to change her clothes, knowing they were on their way in now, she washed her hands and grabbed her lab coat off its hook by the door and walked over to the clinic to get things laid out in case she needed to do emergency surgery on the dog. God, she hoped the rescue guy wasn't going to go all squeamish on her if she needed an extra set of hands. Her ex certainly had the time or two she'd encountered an injured animal during her travels. Then she rolled her eyes. Of course he wouldn't. He was search and rescue. Not a baseball player who was worried more about his pitching arm than anything else. Including the damage he could have done to her reputation if he'd succeeded in using her key.

Fifteen minutes later, she heard a car drive up, horn giving two sharp beeps as it parked in her small gravel lot.

She met them at the door, her breath catching at the man who carried what looked to be a very large bloodhound. The man's black hair was sticking up in every direction, and he had blood caked on the right side of his face, and there was still more flowing from a deep gash on his cheek.

Needed stitches. Her brain was already processing what she saw. "What happened?"

"He fell quite a distance. Landed on a thick branch which went all the way through his right hind leg." The man was out of breath, probably injured himself. Had he fallen as well?

There was another man behind him. "Let me take him, Cabe, dammit. You can barely walk."

"I'm fine. I've got him." His tone brooked no argument.

Running to open the door for the pair, she motioned them into an exam room. "Set him here."

Gingerly setting the injured dog on the table, the man waited as Jessie unwound her stethoscope from her neck, murmuring little words of reassurance to the hound. She'd long learned that the words themselves didn't matter, it was the tone that either soothed or caused fear. When the dog lifted his head to look at her, she held out her hand, fingers curled in so he could sniff it. "That's a good boy. Let's see where you hurt."

His head flopped back onto the table, long ears akimbo, as if exhausted. He probably was. As was his owner if that's who he was. "Whose dog is he?"

"Mine. His name is Soldier."

She blinked. Okay, that was an unusual name. But then his owner seemed a little unusual himself. She looked at him. "Are *you* okay?"

"I'm fine. Just see to him. Please."

The last word had been added in a tone that sounded slightly strangled, belying his gruff manner. He was worried. As any owner would be.

He turned to his companion. "Thanks, Doug. I can take it from here. Go home to your family."

"I'll help you get him home. He weighs a ton."

"I don't think so." She looked up after listening to the dog's heart. "I'd rather he spent the night here." For some reason the words sounded funny to her ears, so she added, "Soldier, I mean. I don't want him moving around, and it's already six o'clock. Unless you need your friend to stay to help me with my exam. It's just me tonight, I'm afraid. And you look…"

"He looks like hell. I've told him that several times already, but you'll find Cabe is as bullheaded as they come." Doug's face softened. "And that dog means everything to him."

She watched as Cabe fixed him with a look that would melt lead. "I'm fine. Go home, Doug."

Doug held up his hands. "I'm going, I'm going. But call me and let me know how he's doing."

"I will."

With that, Doug waved goodbye to her and headed out the door.

Then those steely blue eyes fixed themselves on her face. "Now tell me. What do I need to do?"

Fifteen minutes later, they were in the

small surgical area in the back of the clinic. Soldier had gotten a dose of a short-acting anesthesia so she could irrigate his leg and then X-ray him to check for fractures.

Cabe surprised her, by handling everything like a pro, not balking at anything she asked him to do, including helping cut sutures as she tied them off. "You're a paramedic?"

"That's right. Before that, I was a medic in the army. I went to one of the local shelters soon after I got out…and well, the rest is history." He smiled, glancing at his dog.

"Ahh…" The dog's name suddenly made more sense. So did Cabe's skill in the operating room. "That's why you're not put off by the messier parts of medicine."

"I've seen my share of trauma. But this is the first time with Soldier."

"From what I can see, he's going to be fine. One cracked rib that should heal without a problem with some downtime. And no major vessels lacerated, which is a small miracle considering where that branch went through. We normally recommend leaving the object in just in case—"

"The branch was still attached to the bush,

and he was lying on top of it. No way for me to get underneath him to cut it. And we had to drag him up the hill."

She swallowed. Cabe's own injuries suddenly made more sense. "You held him, and they dragged you up."

He gave a short jerk of his head. "They pulled us both up."

Their eyes caught and held for a few seconds, before Jessie hauled hers away and fastened them back on the dog. Where they should be. She bandaged both sides of the wound, affixing the tape to the area she'd clipped before surgery. "Let's put him in a kennel and let him wake up. I've given him an injection for pain, so that should help him be more comfortable."

She hurried to put a fleece blanket in the largest kennel they had before realizing there was no way he was going to fit in there without it hurting him to move in and out of the door. "On second thought, let's just put him in the exam room we were in before this. He should be more comfortable in there."

Before she had to ask, Cabe scooped the dog into his arms as if he weighed nothing. It sent a shiver through her, and she wasn't sure why. The paramedic looked like he was impervious to anything. Even emotions.

Except for that tiny quaver when he'd murmured to the dog before the anesthesia had taken effect.

They got him into the room, and Cabe set him on the fluffy blanket that she'd wound into a circle on the ground. Then she set water down for him. "I don't want to give him food until I'm sure we're not going to need to put him back under."

He frowned again. "How long will that be?"

"Just an hour or two."

"I'll wait with him, if it's all the same to you. You don't need to stay. I can lock up for you, if you'd like."

She tensed, before forcing herself to relax. "I was already planning on waiting with him. But first, I'm going to need you to hop up onto that exam table so I can get a better look at your cheek. Let me just lower the mechanism a bit first, though."

"The cheek's fine. But if you have something for this headache, I'd accept it."

"I have Advil. And that's it." Was she going to tense up every time someone asked for a simple painkiller? Maybe. "And your cheek is not fine, and it wasn't a request. If you want to stay here with him…" She left the sentence hanging. He'd get the meaning.

He glanced at the table as she pushed a foot pedal to bring it down a little. "Is that thing going to hold me?"

"Yes." Even saying the word made her smile, though. The man had to be six-three or six-four, if he was an inch. But he wasn't tall and scrawny looking. Instead, he was filled out in all the right places. The fact that she was just now noticing that made her kind of proud. At least she hadn't ogled him the second he'd walked through the door.

Well, she wasn't going to ruin that record by staring at him now. Gathering some supplies while he got onto the table, wincing as he did, she tilted her head. "Are you sure you don't need to visit the ER and get a few X-rays of your own?"

"I'm sure. Just got a few bumps and bruises." He glanced at his dog, who was still sleeping off his adventures, thanks to the pain meds. "Are you sure Soldier needs to stay here? We haven't been separated since… well in a long time."

"I'm sorry, but I'd feel better if he were here where I can keep an eye on him."

He frowned. "Are you going to spend the night at the clinic?"

"That's the plan. I have a little sleeping area set up in back." She soaked a piece of gauze with antiseptic. "This is going to sting a little."

She gently cleaned the area on his cheek. She was right. It was fairly deep. "This looks like it needs stitches."

"Okay."

The gauze went still. "So you'll go have it seen?"

"Can't you do it?"

"I'm a vet. Not a human doctor."

His mouth twisted. "Okay… Doc. If I trusted you with Soldier, I sure as hell trust you to knot a few sutures on me. But if you won't, and you have a couple of butterflies or some superglue I can use, I'll just close it myself."

Was he kidding her? Then again, he'd been a medic in the army, he'd probably had to make do with what he had more than once.

"I'll close it with a butterfly bandage. But

you're probably going to have a scar if you don't get it done right."

He actually cracked a smile. "It won't be my first one."

The man was ridiculous. Not only because of what he'd said, but because now she was wondering where those other scars might be hidden.

She switched to a fresh gauze and cleaned up some more superficial cuts on his temple. "Let me check your head."

Her fingers tunneled deep into his dark hair and sifted through the crisp strands as she felt for other injuries or telltale signs of a head injury. No bumps that she could find. He pulled back with a weird sound. "I think I'm fine. If you could just patch up the spot on my cheek, I'll be good to go." He seemed to think for a minute. "Are you sure I can't sleep in your spare room at the clinic so that you can go home to be with…whoever needs you."

Not a chance in hell.

"That would be my bird, Dumble. And I live right next door, so I'll run home to feed him. I'll be gone all of five minutes."

She'd lost her dog, Chloe, to cancer, before

leaving San Francisco. It was part of what had prompted her to move to Santa Medina. She'd had Chloe ever since she was a junior in high school and losing her had been harder than breaking it off with her long-term boyfriend, Jason. Of course finding him with the keys to her drug cabinet and suddenly realizing why Chloe's pain meds had run out much sooner than she'd expected had left her reeling. Jason had been stealing them. At first he denied it. Then claimed he hadn't wanted to go to the doctor for a shoulder injury, he'd told her. None of which she now believed. Nor had she believed his story of finding her keys beside her car and picking them up to return to her. If he'd actually made it to the vet clinic where she worked and stolen drugs… She would have been finished. Anger washed over her all over again.

No. She wasn't trusting anyone the way she'd trusted him, ever again. That included letting someone sleep in her clinic.

"Dumble, huh? No cats or dogs?"

His words jerked her back to the present. "Not anymore."

He frowned and looked at her for a long moment before murmuring, "I'm sorry."

An unexpected wave of emotion overcame her, and a half shrug was all she could get out for several minutes. She hadn't even been able to grieve Chloe's loss properly because of the drama with Jason soon afterward.

She covered by cleaning up the discarded gauze and putting away the disinfectant. Then she pulled out a small, covered tote that held various Band-Aids and found a couple of butterflies. She also retrieved a couple of ibuprofen.

Affixing one side of the dressing and then pulling the edge of the skin to meet with the skin on the other side of the cut, she finished up and stood back to look. "Make sure you have it checked if there's any sign of infection. And you should probably get a tetanus shot if you haven't had one in a while."

She went to the small fridge around the corner and got a bottle of water, then handed it to him along with the ibuprofen.

He twisted the cap and put the bottle to his mouth, downed the pills with a powerful movement of his throat. "Thanks." He slid off the table. "Is that it?"

"Yep, I think we're all done. Go home. Please. He'll probably sleep most of the night, and you look about done in. I'll call you if there's any change."

"Are you sure?"

"Absolutely." A frisson of relief went through her that he was about to be out of her clinic. Something about him made her uneasy. Not in a creepy way, but in a way that said she wasn't sure of her own reactions. And it was strange. Jason had been stunningly attractive with a runner's body and a great sense of humor. And not a scar in sight. But Cabe…there was something darker about this man. More closed off. As if he had a million secrets tucked away behind those blue eyes of his.

He was a combat medic. Who wouldn't have a darker side after that kind of career? Or secrets.

Then again, so had Jason. And none of them had been the good kind.

He patted his vest pockets before shaking his head. "My wallet's in the car…let me get it."

"We can settle up tomorrow when you come get him."

"Are you sure?" As he turned toward her,

his hand knocked the leash she'd used onto the floor.

"I'm sure."

He bent over to pick up the neon-green length of nylon, and Jessie's eyes widened, a shocked squeak coming out before she could stop it.

Because a section of jeans that should have been covering his ass was now a useless flap of fabric that hung to one side, and there, in all its glory, was half of the man's butt, bared for her viewing pleasure. And the knotted muscles there...

Oh, God! Stop looking, stop looking, stop...

She swallowed hard and stared at the wall over his head, waiting for him to turn around.

CHAPTER TWO

THE SOUND THAT came from behind him made him straighten slowly and glance toward Soldier, thinking the dog had done something that had alarmed the vet. But the canine was still resting on his side, snoring slightly.

He turned around. "Are you okay?"

"Your, um…" Her hand did this funny swirly thing in the air and then she patted her backside.

What the hell?

He frowned, having no idea what she was talking about. He reached around to that area on his own anatomy and felt his vest. His head tilted sideways, the movement stretching the skin under the butterfly and making it burn.

"No. Not there. Underneath that coat thing." She pulled off her lab coat and held it by her side, revealing a snug brown T-shirt with just a hint of cleavage visible above the V-shaped neckline. She had a smudge of dirt on her right upper arm. "I have a feeling you might want this."

He was pretty sure his eyes might have burst free of their sockets, before he realized she wasn't referring to her body, but to the white coat which she was now holding out.

"I don't understand."

Her brows went up and a trace of a smile curved the edges of pink lips. "Just. Feel. Your. Ass."

Feel his…?

What the hell? He felt the area again, this time reaching under his vest. His hand met bare skin. The skin of his…ass.

Well, damn.

That's what that cute squeaking noise had been about. His worn jeans must have ripped apart as he was being dragged up the hill holding onto Soldier. Seeing as his buddies hadn't ragged on him about it, it must not have been visible because of his hiking vest…until he bent over. Right in front of the brand-new vet.

Fire marched up his neck and his head

pounded until he thought it might explode. Grinding his teeth, he forced the tide back. He was being ridiculous. It wasn't as if no one had ever seen his backside before, but it also wasn't something he wanted to foist onto someone without them being aware of it…and wanting it.

"Sorry. I didn't realize." He looked at the lab coat she held out. "But I doubt that is going to fit me. Do you have a surgical drape I can use by any chance?"

"Yes…er…just a minute." She discarded her coat on the front desk and went into the back before coming back with a square blue piece of paper. And *her* backside was completely covered by black denim jeans, which hugged every curve.

Damn. He'd come into the clinic assuming that the Jessie Swinton DVM who would emerge was going to be an older man, kind of like Doc Humphrey had been. She was about as far from that image as one could get. She looked like she was nineteen, only there was no way she could be that young. Besides, Doc had been his vet ever since he got back from the army. He'd watched Cabe go through his divorce and the aftermath.

That break hadn't been quick or easy. But he'd seen it coming down the road long before she finally uttered the word *divorce*.

He wasn't sure how he felt about another vet taking his place, even though the man's hands had developed a slight tremor that probably marked the end of his career.

There were other vets, but to change just because Dr. Swinton was different from his last one would be…stupid. How about changing due to embarrassment?

Also stupid.

Besides, it was worth a little bit of a red face as long as it meant Soldier was going to be okay. He realized she was still holding the paper drape. Taking it from her, he tucked it into the back of his jeans, letting it hang behind him like some kind of ridiculous kilt. "Thanks again for coming in and taking care of him after hours."

"Of course. Thanks for assisting, since my only lab tech just went out of town for the weekend."

"Fishing?" When she nodded, he smiled. "Margo does like to fish."

"You know her?"

He nodded. "I grew up around these parts and besides, Margo was also Doc's assistant."

"Does everyone just call him Doc?"

"As far as I know." Belatedly, he realized it might bother her that the town treated the previous veterinarian with such affection. "He grew up in Santa Medina too."

She smiled, the warmth of it washing away some of the sting of being caught with his pants down—or at least a piece of them. "Is there anyone here who *wasn't* raised in this town?"

It was on the tip of his tongue to say "you," but he had a feeling it might make her feel like an outsider, and that's not what he would mean, so he simply said, "People come through all the time. Some stay. Some don't."

And that didn't sound much better, but he suddenly didn't seem to be thinking straight, so names of specific people had eluded him.

He reached in his vest and pulled out yet another business card. "Here's my number. It's my cell. Just call if you need anything or if Soldier does."

"Thanks." She took it from him. "Sorry about not looking you up on the computer, but Margo hadn't shown me how to work all of that yet."

"Not a problem." He crouched down next to his dog, glad of the drape, since he didn't want to make the same mistake a second time. Stroking the hound's soft ears, he drew a deep breath, realizing how badly today could have gone. Randolf could have really had a gun and could have hurt himself or someone else. And Soldier could have died in that fall. But none of that had happened, and hopefully the man would get the help he needed. "Well, boy, I'll be back tomorrow to get you. Don't give Dr. Swinton any problems, okay?"

His pup's eyes rolled around in their sockets for a second, but they didn't really open. Cabe frowned for a second. "I don't know if he hit his head on the way down or not."

"I'll keep an eye on him. I promise." As he stood to his feet, she continued. "He was very lucky. You both were."

"Yes, we were." He looked at her again. "Thank you for letting us come in on your day off."

"It wasn't a problem. I was just out working in the garden."

He smiled. "I thought maybe you were doing something like that." He touched his arm, mimicking what she'd done earlier. "You have something right there."

She glanced down and then laughed, the sound ringing with amusement. "It figures. You're lucky it isn't worse."

"I know. You could be missing part of your clothes."

She blinked for a second and then laughed "Yes. And I can see how that would be much, much worse."

No. Not worse. But much more dangerous. And something he didn't need to be thinking about. Now. Or ever. So he said goodbye and reached down to give Soldier one more pat, promising he'd be here whenever she was ready to send him home and thanking her again for everything.

"Even this." He fingered his cheek, where the butterfly dressings made their presence known every time he smiled.

"I hope you found who you were looking for."

He hesitated. "Yes, I did. See you tomorrow."

As he left the clinic her words came back

to him. "I hope you found who you were looking for."

He knew she'd been talking about the rescue, but for a split second he thought she'd been talking about relationships. He'd thought he'd found who he was looking for in Jackie, his ex. But in the end, the couple who'd been voted most likely to marry in high school had indeed married. Only it hadn't lasted. He'd married her right before shipping out with the army. But once he came home from his...

Well, things had changed.

He climbed in his car and started the engine, glancing at the vet clinic with its Closed sign in full view. As he pulled away, he could have sworn he saw the curtains in the front window twitch. But when he looked again, they were in the same spot they had been. Must have been his imagination. But man, that had been nothing like his interactions with Doc had been.

And he wasn't sure how he felt about that.

Cabe felt like he'd been hit by a Mack truck. Every bone in his body hurt, and he had bruises everywhere. And his shoulder was killing him.

He figured he'd be a little sore today from how hard it had been to get his clothes off last night. His ripped jeans had gone straight in the trash. But the word *sore* didn't describe what he felt like today. He'd tried to call the vet clinic before going into work, but there'd been no answer. It was supposed to have been his day off, but one of his fellow paramedics had called in sick. Cabe probably should have said he couldn't do it. But his nature was to gut it out no matter how hard things got.

Except with Jackie, evidently, although the decision hadn't been his by that time. And he couldn't really blame her. He knew who he was, and despite her best efforts, he hadn't been able to shake his past.

He didn't want Dr. Swinton to be stuck babysitting Soldier today, so he'd hoped to catch her early and pick his boy up before work. He hoped things were okay.

She would have called him if there was a problem, right? She'd promised.

Maybe another emergency case had come in. He hoped not, although first responders never quite knew when those calls would come in either. Like today.

He got to the station, parking around back. But when he went through the doors, he saw the man from yesterday standing in the kitchen area talking to a couple of the other guys. Next to him stood a young woman.

"Randolf?" He stepped around so the man could see him. "Everything okay?"

"Yes, it's okay. I just wanted to come by and say thank you again. If you hadn't found me yesterday…" Randolf paused. "Wow. Are *you* okay?"

Evidently he looked as awful as he felt. "I'm fine."

His wife gripped the man's arm as if afraid he'd disappear if she let go of him. "Yes, thank you." She frowned. "I heard your dog was injured, I'm so sorry. Will he be okay?"

Her voice was so soft he almost didn't hear her. "Yes. Doc… I mean the new vet, got him all patched up. He's still there for observation, and she's taking good care of him."

At least that was his hope.

"Can we do anything? Pay for his care?"

"Search and rescue provides emergency insurance for him. It should cover it. I'm just glad everything turned out the way it did." And that Randolf's resolve to do himself harm had faltered as he realized just what he stood to miss out on.

She smiled. "We're actually on our way to see a counselor. But Randolf insisted on stopping by to see if he could thank you in person. Are the other two men here?"

"No, Doug and Brad are off today, but I'll pass your message along."

Randolf reached out and shook Cabe's hand. "Give my best to Soldier. I'd like to send him over a box of treats, if that's okay."

That made him smile. The man sure sounded better than he had yesterday. "I'm sure he would love that. Come by and let us know how you're doing when you get a chance."

"Thanks. I will." He glanced at his wife. "We'd better get going."

"Yes." She smiled at Cabe. "I can't express how—"

"You don't have to. It was my pleasure. Just take care of each other."

He hadn't been able to rescue his dad from his own demons, but this kind of rescue he could do. Not emotional rescue, but physical rescue. Where you could save a person's life. The rest was up to them. Maybe there was a little part of him that saw it as doing what he hadn't been able to when he was a kid.

Randolf's wife nodded. "We will."

They left just as Sam Murray handed him a wide-rimmed bowl that held some chili and corn bread. "Thanks. How old is this stuff?"

Sam grinned. "Ha! No, my wife took pity on us after that last canned stew incident and made a big pot of chili. From scratch."

The stew had sat on a shelf in the squad's pantry long past its expiration date. After it was heated up on the stove, there'd been no takers when it came to eating it. Not even Sam, who'd been the one to dump it into the pot. But you never knew when a call was going to come in, so there wasn't always time to do a lot of real cooking.

He had to admit, despite his achy joints, the food smelled wonderful. "Well, tell her thank you for me."

"You've got it."

Clay, another of the firefighters, was already at the table digging in. "Are you sure she doesn't want to join the squad?"

"I'm lucky she lets me come in as often

as I do." Sam was nearing retirement age, but you'd never know it from his youthful appearance.

Just as Cabe took his first bite, his phone went off. He glanced at the readout and frowned, then held up a finger to the two men. "I'll be back in a sec. Nobody touch that bowl."

Walking a short distance away, he answered. "Is he okay?"

"He's fine. I told you I'd call if he wasn't."

Her voice was soft and lilting with no hint of irritation over the fact that he'd tried to reach her twice. "Sorry for the calls. I wanted to let you know I got called in to work unexpectedly but will try to work out a time to come get him sometime this morning. Is he okay hanging out at the clinic for a little while longer?"

"No hurry. I didn't want to leave him locked in the exam room, so he's actually following me around the yard. Glad I don't have any bodies buried out here. He's been nose-to-the-ground the whole time."

That made him chuckle. "He loves his job. How about his leg?"

"He's limping but getting around okay. I don't think there will be any permanent damage to the muscle or nerves. He was very lucky."

Lucky. That word seemed to be thrown around a lot.

Before he could say anything, she said, "Well, I just called with an update. No hurry coming by. But I would like to know what he normally eats for breakfast and how much."

"Oh, of course." He named the brand of food that he normally gave Soldier and the amount. "But if you don't have it, I'm sure he'll be fine with whatever you've got on hand. But don't let him sweet-talk you into giving him more than his portion. He'll make you think he hasn't eaten in forever."

She laughed. "Oh, I can see he's well fed. In a good way. His weight is perfect. How's the offending cheek?"

"Pardon me?"

"Your cheek… Oh! I mean the one on your face."

Dammit. Of course she had. What was wrong with him?

"It's fine. The butterflies are holding.

Thanks for agreeing to do them…and for the ibuprofen. I was beat yesterday."

And why had he said that? She didn't care if he was tired or not.

He was going to need to tread carefully around Dr. Swinton. His ex had laid things out about as clearly as she could. He was not good husband material—although she'd seemed to like him well enough in high school. Except the "I love my bad boy" endearments she used to whisper during lovemaking had shifted to shrill accusations that he was emotionally stunted and unavailable. And he had to agree with her. He'd probably no business getting married to her…or to anyone. But he'd convinced himself that he'd be able to do it: that despite the scars from his dad, he'd still be able to connect with someone on an emotional level and sustain a relationship. How wrong he'd been.

He wasn't going to put anyone else through what he'd put her through.

"I'm sure you were. Hope you're feeling better today."

Not really. Although he was glad Randolf and his wife appeared to be headed down the right path. At least counseling would work for someone. He'd suggested counseling to Jackie, thinking it was the expected thing to do, even though his heart wasn't in it. But she hadn't even wanted to try. To say he'd been relieved was an understatement. And once she walked out, he'd canceled the appointment. Maybe that made him a hypocrite for making Randolf promise to go see someone. But then again, Randolf wasn't him.

"I'm fine. I'm glad to hear Soldier is up and moving around though. Sorry for not being able to come get him right now."

"He's good company, actually. So no hurry. Just let me know when you're on your way, so I can meet you at the clinic."

"I will. And thanks again."

"See you in a while."

He sighed, not sure seeing her again was something that was smart, but it was necessary.

"Hopefully it won't be too long. I'll call you."

"Yes. Do that." And with that, his phone showed that she'd already hung up.

What was she doing at home that had Soldier following her around? More gardening? Somehow picturing her digging in the garden with a spade, another smear of dirt on her arm, and maybe one across her forehead made his gut tighten in a way that he didn't like. Well, he'd better get himself together and start concentrating on work and figure out when he could go get Soldier and take him home.

Because the sooner he went to pick his dog up, the better. Before there was any more mention of his cheek. The one on his face or any other one.

Jessie was nervous. Not because of Soldier— who was doing fine—but because she'd just had the idea of the century. Or at least the idea of the last fifteen minutes. And she had Cabe to thank for it, since it turned out that Soldier was a shelter dog. But she wasn't sure he would go for it. Or if she should even ask. But one of the things she'd hoped to carry over from her last job was the series of community education seminars about how having a pet can benefit not just the person who owns them, but also the community at large. The seminars had always been a big hit in San Francisco.

She'd already called one of the animal

shelters and they were on board with doing a seminar on pet adoption, and they were planning on bringing some of their charges with them. But how great would it be to have someone in the search and rescue field— who'd adopted his dog from a shelter—talk about what it entails and the type of training their dog undergoes.

Cabe was due at the clinic any minute. And she was perched precariously on a step-ladder trying to get the stupid battery-powered screwdriver to cooperate.

Soldier gave a low woof as if commiserating with her.

"I know. The stupid angle isn't helping any, boy." The driver slipped yet again, and this time hit her thumb, and the screw fell to the floor. "Dammit!"

"Something I can do to help?"

Her head whipped around so fast that she teetered on the ladder and would have fallen, if warm hands hadn't landed on her hips.

Oh, God. Of all the stupid…

"Sorry." The man was basically holding her in place, and there was nothing to grab onto to pull herself back upright.

Before she could try to figure it out, he

lifted her feet free of the ladder and set her down on the ground. She swallowed, the picture of him cradling his dog sliding back through her head. Those muscles weren't just for show. Although it made sense if he had to go on rescue missions.

Turning toward him so she wasn't tempted to lean into his touch, she bit her lip. "Talk about clumsy."

"I startled you. I should be the one apologizing."

Looking at him though, he didn't look the least bit sorry. In fact there was a ghost of a smile on the man's face. The darkness she'd sensed in him yesterday was nowhere to be seen right now. And she found she liked that. It made her more optimistic about what she wanted to ask him.

Soldier wound around them, tongue hanging out with excitement. "He's barely limping at all now. I think he's happy to see you."

"I'm pretty happy myself. There was a time yesterday when I thought…" His voice faded. She could imagine where his thoughts had gone.

"He's fine, as you can see. I gave him a

pain pill this morning, but it should be wearing off by now."

"Do I need to give him something when I get him home?" His hands went onto his lean hips, perching there in a totally sexy way that made her mouth go dry.

Her so-called brilliant idea suddenly didn't seem quite as wise as it had a little while ago.

"I want him to continue the antibiotics. One pill a day, but unless he seems uncomfortable, let's hold off on the pain pills. I'll send two home with you. They can affect his motility. I mean—"

"I know what you mean."

She wasn't sure how to say this, but really felt it needed to be made clear. "If you don't have to give him the pills, I'd appreciate it if you returned them to me so I can dispose of them."

His head tilted as he looked at her. "The antibiotics?"

"No. The carprofen."

"Not a problem. I know they shouldn't be flushed."

Her muscles went slack all at once. Why had she said that? Was she seriously going to ask every client to return unused pain meds?

No. But something inside her had blurted the words before she could stop herself.

Before she could try to come up with a logical explanation, he motioned at the bulletin board on the wall that was sitting askew, since it only had one screw in it. "What's this?"

Well, if she was going to do it, she needed to do it now.

"At my last clinic, we had a series of educational seminars on pets in the community. So far I have one of the local shelters scheduled to speak on their community ambassador program." She cleared her throat. "You wouldn't be interested in bringing Soldier in and talking about your and his work in search and rescue, would you?"

His hand reached down to his dog and fingered his ear as if needing time to figure out how to politely decline her offer.

She hurried to say, "I mean, I'll understand if you don't have time between your job and everything, so please don't feel pressured to say yes. It's just that it would be great for people to see that shelter dogs can bring so much benefit to society at large."

"I think it's a great idea. I don't think Doc

had anything like this when he was here. How often are you thinking?"

"Once a week was what we did in San Fran. Search and rescue, though, I think would be a big draw. If you had the time, you could take two or even three sessions. And if you know of someone who trains dogs to do what Soldier does, that would be a great way to close out the subject, in case anyone might want to pursue that line of work or get involved."

"It's harder to get people involved in SAR when it's not a paid position."

She frowned. "You volunteer?"

"Yes. I should clarify that I get paid for being a paramedic, but not for my work with SAR. I help when I'm available."

That surprised her. "You must really love it, then."

"Soldier definitely does." He paused. "Which makes me ask. Will he continue to have problems with his leg even after it's healed? Do I need to think about retiring him?"

"I don't see why he wouldn't be able to go back to work. He's limping now, just because the muscle is sore. Unless there are unforeseen complications, he should be as right as rain in a few weeks." She smiled. "From what I saw of him, retirement wouldn't suit him."

Or you. The words hung on the tip of her tongue, but she didn't say them. After all, she really didn't know him. At all.

And that wasn't likely to change, even if he agreed to participate in the seminar program.

Cabe took the screwdriver from her and picked up the screw that had fallen to the floor. Without asking, he stepped onto the lowest rung of the ladder and finished securing the bulletin board to the wall. The man was definitely tall. She'd almost been on the top of the ladder and had still had to stretch up to reach it. She hadn't wanted it to hang so low that little kids or large dogs might be able to reach the tacks. "How's that?"

"It's great, thanks."

He stepped off the ladder and handed her the screwdriver. "What day of the week are the seminars on?"

She'd half expected him to come up with an excuse of why he couldn't participate, but so far, he hadn't.

"Right now, I have them planned for Saturdays. But I can be flexible."

"Let me see if I can get two Saturdays in a row off, although I don't think it will be a problem. Which weeks do you want me to take?"

She blinked. "You mean you'll do it?"

"It certainly sounds that way."

She smiled. "Great! Since I only have the shelter signed up so far, and they're coming this week, do you think you can do the following Saturday and the one after that?"

"Let me double-check with the station, but I'm pretty sure I can trade with someone, if I'm scheduled. After all it's the least I can do to repay you."

That threw her. "Repay me?"

"For not letting me walk out that door yesterday knowing what you did. I'd planned on going to the pharmacy for some painkillers, and I wouldn't have wanted to be on...display. So you saved me both the trip and the embarrassment."

Oh! She got it. Motioning to the ladder, "I think you just repaid me by not letting me crash to the ground."

He grinned. "So we're even?" He pulled

his wallet from his pocket. "Except for the emergency vet service that is. I have Soldier's insurance card."

She waved him away. "I'll donate that in exchange for your expertise in doing the seminar." In case he was thinking of arguing with her, she added, "I'm donating services to the shelter as well, in exchange for them coming to speak."

This time it was Cabe who frowned. "You'll go out of business pretty quickly if you keep giving away services. Seriously, though, I don't know what I would have done if you couldn't see Soldier. The next clinic is thirty miles away, and I didn't want him to have to wait that long."

"Of course! I'm happy I was home."

They both stood there for a minute or two in silence. Then Soldier nudged at Cabe's hand, and he drew in a quick breath, his demeanor seeming to change instantly. "I think he's hinting that he's ready to go home. I'll confirm my participation in the seminar."

It wasn't her imagination that he suddenly didn't sound as enthused as he had moments earlier about doing it. But that was on him.

If he didn't want to, he could speak up and say so.

"Thanks for considering it." Her fingers reached up to touch his injured cheek before she had time to think. When his brows went up, she hurried to say, "This looks better. It's not as puffy today."

"It feels pretty good, all things considered. Thanks again for putting me back together."

Except she had a feeling she hadn't. And whether or not what she'd sensed was part of her imagination or something very real, she'd treated enough sick and injured animals to know that some living creatures couldn't be put back together. Not by her. Not by anyone. Just like Jason.

Knowing where that line was was an important part of her job in alleviating suffering. But not with humans. That wasn't her job. And certainly not with this man. The sooner she remembered that, the better off she would be.

CHAPTER THREE

TWO DAYS LATER, Cabe walked out of the small office in the fire department that housed the Santa Medina Search and Rescue Center and rolled his eyes. Not only did his boss think that taking part in Jessie's seminar series was a good idea, he wanted to go all out and put on a demonstration of all it entailed. And that meant that Cabe had to set up a mock rescue of another team member, have Soldier find him, and then climb down to "save" him. His banged-up shoulder still hurt like anything, so the prospect of climbing didn't thrill him all that much.

Was that the only reason?

No.

Startling Jessie and having to almost catch her had done a number on his nerves. He'd found himself reliving that scene in microseconds over the last couple of days. He'd almost…almost…turned her toward him and…

And what? Kissed her?

Oh, he was sure *that* would have been well received. Not. His mouth twitched sideways. He'd also imagined the possibilities of the aftermath of that kiss in stunning detail. And some of those possibilities had been…

But "the kiss that wasn't" wasn't the only thing that bothered him about that day. Cabe had stood there chatting with her as if she were an old friend. It had felt warm and comfortable. Something he hadn't felt in a long time.

But Jessie was not a friend. And he wasn't even sure why he'd gotten so worked up over lifting her off that ladder. He hadn't kissed her, although the urge had certainly been there.

He could only chalk it up to gratefulness over the way she'd taken care of Soldier, taking his dog home with her and letting him follow her around.

And now he had to call her and tell her what Terry had said about the seminar. Maybe she wouldn't want anything that in-depth and would say "thanks but no thanks" to anything but the informational talks, although she'd seemed keen to let him do as much or as little as he felt comfortable with. Well, his comfort level was pretty much nil at the moment.

Maybe he could pass the job off to Brad or Doug. He rolled his eyes, remembering that she wanted to show how *"companion animals"* as in shelter animals helped the community. It wasn't just about SAR. And Soldier was the only search and rescue dog in this area, although there were others they could call on if there was a massive search effort underway, just like he and Soldier could go and help another team if they were ever needed.

He opened the back door to his car to let Soldier jump in, noting the dog's leg and ribs weren't giving him any trouble, before going around and climbing into his own seat. Only then did he dial the number to the clinic. In the back seat, Soldier gave an enthusiastic bark, anxious to be on their way.

She answered it on the first ring. "Santa Medina Veterinary Clinic, may I help you?"

"Jessie? It's Cabe." Surprised that he'd recognized her voice instantly, he'd forgotten to use her title. If she noticed she didn't let on. "Did Margo not make it back yet?"

"She did. She's just on her lunch break. How's Soldier doing?"

"He's great. Barely even a limp." It had been two days since the injury, and it was looking better each day. Like his cheek.

"That's great news. So if you're not calling about Soldier…"

"Do you have a patient right now?"

"Nope. Do you want to come over?"

Maybe this would be better done in person. Then he could gauge the reaction on her face. If there was any hesitation, he would gladly scale his participation down to a simple speech, with Soldier standing next to him. "Sure. It won't take long, I promise."

"You're not going to speak, are you."

It took him a second before he realized she was talking about the seminar itself and not about her wanting him to remain silent when he arrived at the clinic.

"No, I am. It's just…" He thought fast. "Do you have time for a coffee?"

There was a pause. "How about if I put

a pot on at the house. Then you can tell me whatever it is that's on your mind."

That was probably a better solution. "Are you done for the day?"

"Pretty much. Barring any unforeseen emergencies."

He and Soldier had been one of those. "I have Soldier with me, is that a problem?"

"I already know he doesn't gobble up birds so no, it's not a problem."

That made him smile. "Okay, we'll be there in about twenty minutes, if that's not too soon."

"I should be just about ready for you by then."

The words sent a shard of something through him. According to his ex no one was ready to deal with him. And she was probably right. He'd never seemed to be good at relationships…whether they were familial or romantic.

Which basically ruled out relationships in general, except with his mom. And even their relationship wasn't the best in the world, although it was certainly better than it used to be. Mainly because she'd finally realized that she had an issue with codependency, getting involved with men she thought she could heal. Only it never worked out. Not with his dad. Not with the three other relationships she'd had since then.

But thank God she'd booted the last guy out. Now if she could just keep it that way.

His ex had basically booted his butt to the curb for the same reason. He wasn't a drunk. But growing up with one had made him guarded with his feelings. Not the ideal kind of person to be with if you wanted emotional intimacy. Which Cabe didn't. Not anymore.

Starting up the car, he pulled out of the space and headed toward the clinic.

Jessie's house still looked like Doc's. Probably because she'd just moved in not that long ago. Except there was a huge birdcage in the middle of the living room. What was—unfortunately—*not* in the cage, was a huge white cockatoo.

This was her bird? He'd pictured something…well, smaller. Less threatening.

As it was, the feathered creature was sitting on a large perch that was just about at face level.

The better to peck your eyes out.

Cabe had never been around birds, not even chickens, so he stared at it warily.

The bird's head twisted sideways and tilted as if studying them. When he saw Soldier, his comb went up and he stepped with funny jerky movements along his perch, moving closer to the intruders. "Nice doggy." The singsong words were followed by a whistle that was definitely not politically correct.

Cabe thought his brows were going to shoot straight off his forehead.

"Dumble! That's not nice."

The bird repeated the whistle, then said, "Not nice. Dumble not nice."

The cockatoo didn't sound in the least sorry for what he'd done.

"Oh, jeez." Jessie's face colored. "I'm sorry. I can't seem to break him of that."

"I take it you didn't teach him that."

"Nope. That definitely wasn't me. I sort of inherited him. I did a stint in vet school studying exotic birds, and one of my professors died midyear. It was terrible. Dumble was his. He had nowhere to go, and so I…"

"Inherited him. Did you inherit his name too?"

Jessie certainly seemed to be a softy when it came to animals. Which made sense.

"Yep. My professor said his kids had grown up with a children's book series and they'd named him. Dumble's close to twenty-five years old now." She smiled. "Anyway, come in and sit down. I have the coffee made. How do you take it?"

He moved further into the room and sat on a sofa that had to be the same age as the bird. The upholstery was dark beige with kind of a velvety texture. It did not fit Jessie—or her bird—at all.

As if reading his thoughts, she smiled. "I haven't had a chance to redecorate yet. And I'm more of an outdoor girl than an indoor one. Working in the garden seemed prefer-able to replacing all of the furnishings in the house."

Dumble had swiveled on the perch, con-tinuing to eye Soldier and Cabe in a way that made him slightly uneasy. "He won't come down and visit us, will he?"

She gave him a funny look. "You don't like birds?"

He shrugged. "I've never really been around them."

"Don't worry about him. He's harmless. And he's not a spring chicken anymore. I can put him in his cage, if you want, though."

"No. It's okay." Soldier had flopped down onto the floor, his injured leg facing up, and seemed totally unconcerned about a possible visit from Dumble. If his dog wasn't worried, then he wouldn't be either. "Can I help with the coffee?"

"Nope. I'll get it." She paused. "I don't think you ever told me how you take it?"

"Just black."

"Of course you do," she muttered, then as if she hadn't meant to say the words out loud, she added. "You're kind of a no-frills guy."

The words made him tense. If she only knew how right she was.

He didn't do soft and mushy, or romantic and sweet. Not easily anyway. Oh, he knew what was expected out of a partner, and could occasionally get with the program and do the prescribed flowers and chocolate. But it always felt like an act. Like he was playing a part without really feeling any genuine emotions. And that worried him. His ex had deserved more, and she knew it. But he felt like he didn't have more to give.

Which was why he had sworn off relation-ships. He felt like he had more of his dad in him than he might like to think. And now that he was divorced, he could make a con-scious decision to not be put in that position ever again.

Realizing she was waiting for a response, he said. "You're exactly right. No frills here."

She gave a weird kind of smile and then said, "I'll be right back with the coffee. Dumble...be good." And then she left the room.

"Dumble not good. Dumble not good."

Cabe shot the bird a look. "You're not the only one, pal."

"Not the only one. Not the only one."

Hell, the last thing he needed was to have the bird start repeating what he said. But if there was an off button, he had no idea where it was.

Jessie came back a couple of minutes later with a tray and two heavy white coffee mugs. He wasn't the only one who did no frills, ev-idently. No delicate porcelain cups in sight. She set the coffee on the table in front of the sofa and handed him a mug.

Dumble squawked and then parroted. "Not

the only one." He repeated the phrase a few more times.

The veterinarian frowned at her bird. "Sometimes I have no idea where he comes up with these things."

Cabe busied himself taking a drink of coffee, to avoid commenting, while she sat in the chair across from him. Soldier's tail thumped a time or two, although the dog didn't open his eyes. He was asleep on the rug.

Her lab coat was long gone. Instead, she had on jeans and a black tank top, its narrow straps showing off her shoulders to perfection. Something he shouldn't be noticing. And her wavy blond tresses were pulled back in a high ponytail, making her neck look incredibly long. Incredibly kissable.

Coming here had been a bad idea.

Oblivious to his thoughts, she glanced at the dog and then at him. "He looks like he's doing pretty well." She nodded at him and then added, "And your injury seems to be healing."

"It's much better, thanks. I figure seven days, and I can take the butterflies off?"

"About that. Depends on how often you smile."

That made him look at her.

"Sometimes if sutures are in an area of high movement, we leave them in an extra day or two to make sure things are going to hold."

Ah, that made sense. "Well, in my case, seven days should just about do it." Although he could feel the muscles in his cheek twitch as if trying to pull his lips up. Great. It was as if she'd just said "don't think about the word gorilla" and of course that was impossible to do once the suggestion was made.

"Are you saying you don't smile much?" Before he could answer, she took a drink of her own coffee, staring at him over the rim of her cup. "So, you wanted to talk about the seminar? Were you able to get the time off?"

"Yes, but there's a catch. Kind of a big one."

As expected, he watched her frown before he added, "If you decide it's not what you're looking for, feel free to say so. But just so you know, it wasn't my idea."

"Okay…" She drew the word out slowly. "What's the catch?"

"My boss, actually. To promote our work,

he would like to do a mock rescue on-site at the Stately Pleasure Dome."

She gave him a look. "Pleasure Dome? Okay. I'm not even sure what that is, and I'm a little afraid to ask."

The name was so ubiquitous to the area, that he never even gave it a second thought. But he could see how it sounded to someone who wasn't from the area. Maybe he needed to backtrack a bit. His lips twitched and then he smiled.

"It's kind of an unofficial name for one of the rock formations in the Tuolumne Meadows area."

"I see. It's kind of a weird name."

"The rumor is it was named after a poem. Anyway, it's a popular climbing area, since it's easily accessible."

"And where are the meadows? Too-All-Oh-Me, did you say?"

Another smile at the way she drew out the name. "We're not that far from there, actually. You've never been to Tuolumne Meadows?"

"I'm from San Francisco, remember? I mean, I've researched some of the nearby areas, but since I've only been here a couple of weeks, I haven't had a chance to visit anything."

Of course she hadn't. He'd been stupid to assume otherwise. "Sorry, I should have realized that."

"It's okay." She took another sip of her drink then set the mug on the table. "So what would this mock rescue entail?"

"Soldier would show how he tracks a scent and then once the 'injured hiker' is found, me and three other team members would stage a rescue."

"Would this be one of the two weeks you agreed to present?"

"No, it would probably need to be the week after the presentation. Maybe have anyone interested meet us at the site. Terry— my boss—would like to hand out brochures afterward telling people how to get involved with our team and what's required."

She sat there for a minute before saying, "Wow."

Okay, so he had no idea if she meant that "wow" as in did he really expect her to agree to that? Or a "wow" as in the request was so much more than she'd hoped for.

"So what do you think?"

"I think it's perfect. I feel lucky to be able to see how a rescue takes place."

"Really?"

"Really. I would like to go and visit the site for myself, though, if possible. The accessibility and so forth might be an issue if we have a lot of interest."

He'd really expected she would balk at the idea. Had halfway hoped she would. But instead, there was a gleam of excitement in her eyes.

"Can you tell me how to get there? Or is there an address I could look up?" she asked.

"Maybe it would be better if I just take you there."

And where the hell had that just come from?

"I would love that. When?"

If they were going to do this, it needed to be soon, so his team could plan and figure out what they were going to do. He had no idea why, but part of her enthusiasm was rubbing off on him. They did training sessions all the time, but normally there wasn't an audience. And lately because of the challenges involved in organizations like theirs, there had been talks of financial cutbacks. Most of the team were volunteers, so the savings couldn't be taken out in salaries. Instead, it meant equipment that couldn't be replaced or repaired, and they would have to make do. That meant possibly putting team members in danger.

"Do you have time this week? You said the shelter is taking this coming Saturday, right?"

"Yep." She stood and retrieved her phone from the back pocket of her jeans. "Let me check what I have scheduled for the rest of the week."

She sat back down and ran her finger over the phone screen. "Wednesday is pretty booked. And Thursday. How about Friday? Are you working?"

"I work 1:00 a.m. until nine. Could we meet at the clinic around ten?"

"Are you sure you want to do a field trip after working those kinds of hours?"

He smiled. Cabe actually thrived on the long hours. It gave him less time to think. Or to think too far into the future. A place he didn't really like to visit. "I'm sure. It'll take about thirty minutes to arrive at the Dome.

But it's a nice view and there's a road that runs right beside it."

"Parking?"

"There's some on the road along that area. Even if there's a large group, there'd be less than a quarter-mile walk to get there."

"Sounds perfect." Her smile widened. "Thank you for being willing to participate. I imagine this will pull in quite a few people."

"That's what Terry is hoping. And if we can get some experienced climbers involved that would be ideal. If you have time maybe stop in at the office and meet him before we go. And I'll let him know that you're in agreement with it."

He hadn't been to Tuolumne Meadows as a tourist in years. Strangely, he was looking forward to seeing it through Jessie's eyes. And maybe even looking forward to a little more of her company? That was something he was not going to say anywhere near her bird. The cockatoo appeared to have lost interest in them and looked to be dozing on his perch at the moment. A very good thing.

He stood, finishing the last of his coffee. "Well, we've taken enough of your time. Thanks for the coffee." He looked down at where his dog was looking up at him with expectancy. "You ready to go, boy?"

Soldier leaped up and stood right beside him, waking up Dumble, who turned on his perch to stare at them again.

Cabe reached down and rubbed the dog's head. He took back what he'd thought about emotions. He loved his dog. But then Soldier's expectations of him were fairly low, and there was no prevaricating or hinting or getting upset if Cabe didn't say exactly the right thing. That was the kind of relationship he excelled at. Where things were pretty much mapped out and rarely strayed from the prescribed path. He glanced up at Jessie and something in his chest thumped.

Not so with the woman in front of him. Or any woman, for that matter. In that, he felt totally lost and out of his element when he was around them.

"Not the only one," Dumble mocked.

For some reason, the words made Cabe laugh. "Remind me not to confess to any crimes around him."

"Yes, that would not be good, although I'm not sure how admissible it would be in a court of law. Especially if he started in with his infamous whistle."

She handed the bird a peanut, which he deftly cracked open and ate, dropping the shell onto the papered shelf beneath him. Then she gave him a scratch beneath his beak with the tip of her fingers, which the bird leaned into.

Cabe couldn't blame him. Her ponytail swished as she leaned forward to give the bird a quick kiss.

Something tightened in his gut. A thin thread of longing that he didn't recognize. Didn't want to recognize. And on that note...

"Well, I'll get out of your way. Until Friday?"

She straightened to look at him, tucking a stray lock behind her ear. An image went through Cabe of him being the one tucking that strand back in place. Of leaning forward to...

"Until Friday."

Friday at the Pleasure Dome. Oh, hell, he should have chosen another place. Any other place. For not the first time, he was thinking how stupid it had been to suggest taking her up to Tuolumne.

To survive this, he was going to have to make sure he kept his mind on work and off...

Well, anything else.

CHAPTER FOUR

THE PLACE HE indicated had no cars in front of it, which surprised her. But then again it was before noon and most locals worked on Fridays, Cabe had said.

He'd picked her up from her clinic a half hour ago, and she'd carried most of the conversation on the short trip. Maybe it was nerves, but she had the feeling that's just the way Cabe was. The strong silent type? It appeared that way. But he didn't seem irritated by her chatter, which was a huge relief.

He found a spot right in front of a rock formation and pulled alongside the road. "Well, this is it. The Stately Pleasure Dome."

"Wow. You weren't kidding when you said the road ran directly in front of it." She glanced in the distance and saw several other mounded rock formations scattered throughout a huge flat area. "So is this the meadow you were talking about?"

"Yes, and this is probably the best spot to do the demo. It'll provide a great view of what's going on." He paused. "Since we're only about three weeks out, Soldier should be healed enough to make it up that slope?"

"I think so. Is he limping today?"

"No, and he got into the car fine. I'm not seeing any discomfort in the leg or his ribs."

"Animals heal remarkably fast. Probably because their ancestors had to in order to survive." She peered toward the east side of the formation. "Will the display be on the front side of the rock or in back."

He smiled. "Unless you or your group can walk on water, it'll have to be on this side. I'll take you around and show you why. There's a road around part of it, but there's water on just the other side of it."

Exiting the car, he let Soldier out. The dog immediately started tracking scents. The scent hounds had always fascinated her.

"Does he ever find something you haven't asked him to find?" Jessie followed his lead out and stood on the embankment watching the bloodhound's intent search.

"All kinds of things. He's almost always nose to the ground. I imagine scents are like tastes to us. So many different smells out there to sort through."

Cabe turned to the side, and Jessie couldn't resist letting her glance alight on his butt, where his black jeans covered taut well-muscled flanks. He turned before she was ready for him to, and he caught her. When her face heated, his mouth canted to the side for a second or two. But thank God, he didn't say anything. Maybe because he couldn't be positive about what she'd been looking at.

Hurrying to find another topic, she said, "So how will this work? Is the person who's pretending to be injured going to be on one of those flat areas and you'll climb up to him?"

He put a hand up to shade his eyes and looked at the rock. "Yes, although we haven't decided if I'll be climbing down to him or going up. It depends on what's needed. If someone falls while hiking or mountain climbing, for instance, we might have to climb up one of the main tracts and then descend to their level. Fortunately these domes are popular climbing spots, so there are already bolts left by other climbers that we can anchor to. People have even mapped out the best travel paths."

"I'm not sure what any of that means, since I've never climbed before."

"It means we can get to someone faster than we would if we had to set our own spots to anchor ourselves to."

A shiver went through her as she imagined how it might be to fall from a height and have to wait for someone to come help her. "Got it."

Just then he gave a shrill set of whistles that made Soldier's head come up. He immediately headed their way with a big lumbering trot that made her smile. His long ears were flipping and flopping with every footfall. "Those ears. I just can't get over them."

"He's a pretty special guy."

"I can't imagine how awful it was when he fell."

He blew out a breath. "It was pretty terrible. I expected to climb down and find him either dead or at death's door. But he's a tough one, aren't you, boy." He rubbed the dog's ears when Soldier pulled up next to him.

"How often do you get called out on rescues? Are most of them climbing related?" She'd never actually met anyone involved in SAR. She found she was looking forward to the demonstration at least as much as anyone who might come to watch.

Cabe was so totally different than Jason had been. At least on the surface. As far as what was underneath, who knew. It was hard for her to trust her judgment in that area right now.

Her ex had been a true urbanite at heart, self-assured, soaking up the attention after a successful ball game. He also had no problems expressing himself. She had no doubt he would hate Santa Medina. His passion was baseball and his earnings had been a lot more than hers. She and Chloe and Dumble had lived in one of his posh residences with him for over a year. But Jason had not been a fan of Dumble's incessant talking, and Jessie had chafed at the lack of green space around the building, although the views from his apartment had been breathtaking. Then Chloe had gotten cancer, and Jason had made some unforgiveable choices during that time. Even so, her decision to leave him had been hard. Even now, she could remember the sick churning of emotions as he asked her to give him another chance.

She couldn't afford to. Not with that kind of betrayal.

And she would never put herself in that position ever again. From now on, she was going to guard her heart with as much diligence as she guarded the keys to her medicine cabinet.

And Cabe? He didn't do a whole lot of talking. Nor was he open with his emotions, from what she'd seen of him. But what she had seen were snatches of the deep love and admiration he had for his dog.

But, like Jason, he also didn't seem to be Dumble's biggest fan, although it didn't matter, because she didn't have to live with the man. Nor would she. It had been such a relief to be on her own again after Jason's unconscionable acts, that she couldn't see wanting to change that anytime soon. And if she did, it would be with someone who wanted the same things out of life as she did. Someone she came to trust. And that would only come after years of knowing that person. After years of digging for any secrets that could bring heartache. And honestly, she wasn't sure if she would ever take that leap again.

She blinked the thoughts away, when she realized Cabe had said something to her. "Sorry?"

"I was saying that we can go up onto the lower part of the Dome if you want. We wouldn't need any equipment for that, since the pitches are fairly low key."

"Really? I would love that!"

Although there were mountains accessible in the distance in California, it wasn't something she'd done a whole lot of as a kid, since her parents, like Jason, were pretty much indoor people.

Another car had pulled up and a couple exited with what looked like rugged outdoor gear. Both of them had a variety of bungee cord type thingies clipped onto their belts. Although she wasn't the biggest fan of heights, she could see how rock climbing could be fun. Maybe she'd take a class or two on some of the tamer slopes.

The couple waved to them as they passed by.

"Which slope are you doing?" Cabe asked.

"We're thinking we might head up to the Boltway."

He nodded. "Have a good climb."

"Thanks, we will." The pair went on their way, scrambling up the lower surface of the rock formation before things got steeper. At that point, they began using their hands and the girl pulled something off her belt. One of the bungee-looking things.

"What are those straps?"

"They're climbing slings. They're used to help you anchor to different points during the climb." He peered up at the couple. "Let's go ahead and go up one of the outcroppings where we can sit. I'll explain what our plans are for the demo, and you can see if it'll fit in with what you want."

She smiled. "Oh, I'm sure it will be. You guys are giving me a lot more than I even dared to hope for."

Following Cabe up the slope, she was glad she'd worn tennis shoes rather than sandals. She'd needed the grip of the rubber several times as the terrain's slope increased. When she hesitated for a second, Cabe reached his hand down for her.

Grabbing it, she let him haul her up to the ledge he was standing on. "I can see why people carry all that gear now. This isn't as easy as it looks." And she considered herself to be fairly athletic.

"No, it's not."

Soldier had had a much easier time scrambling up the hill than she had. "He doesn't seem traumatized by his fall."

"No, and I'm very glad he's not hesitating."

Quite the opposite, actually. The dog plopped down on a horizontal stretch of rock that was shaded by an overhang. Cabe took the backpack he'd slung over one of his shoulders and produced two water bottles, handing her one of them.

"Thanks." She definitely hadn't come prepared. She hadn't even thought to bring water. But then again, she hadn't thought she'd be actually scrambling up a slope. She lowered herself onto the rock, which felt surprisingly cool compared to the warm temperatures of the air around them.

Cabe poured a little of his own bottle out into a depression in the rock near the dog, and Soldier lapped it up, without even getting to his feet.

Then he sat down beside her. Another car had parked, and hikers were getting out of it as well. "I bet this place gets congested with climbers on weekends."

"Definitely. And not just on weekends. It's one of the most popular climbs in the area because of how easy the access is."

She looked out over the road and beyond. It was surprisingly quiet. "It's beautiful."

"Yes, it is. The lakeside is even more so."

Soldier stretched out on his side with a sigh of contentment. Chloe would have loved this spot too, although with her little legs, she'd have probably needed to be carried up. The thought that Jason had used some of her pain meds for himself instead of giving them to her still made her heart cramp. It was an ache she'd probably never be rid of.

"I bet the views from the top are spectacular."

"Yes, they are." He glanced at her. "You should take some classes in climbing. You might find you like it."

"I was just thinking that, although I'm kind of terrified of heights."

"You might surprise yourself. I'd stick to the easy slopes at first, though. They have some pretty impressive views as well." His smile reached his butterfly bandage and made lines radiate out beside his eyes. The expression was warm and so genuine that it made her stomach twist.

She found herself smiling back, her gaze moving to take in the snoozing dog. What a perfect day. If she had thought ahead, she could have packed a picnic lunch, although Cabe might have thought she was being presumptuous, if she had, since he'd made no mention of sharing a meal on this trip. "I'll have to make it a point to take in more of the sights. Yosemite is gorgeous, if this is any indication."

"Yes. It's beautiful."

She hesitated, before asking, "Can I look at your butterflies to make sure they're holding up okay?" Although she wasn't sure what she was going to do if they weren't.

His eyes fastened on hers for several seconds. "Go ahead."

Jessie got up on her knees and leaned in to look at the bandages, which weren't quite as white as they'd been when she'd put them on. Her fingers touched his warm cheek and slid to the edge of the first butterfly, her gaze taking in the sealed skin around it. It looked like it was healing well. She tested the edges of the skin. It remained sealed. "It looks just about perfect, I think."

"Yes. It does." His murmur rumbled through her, the tones warm and hypnotic.

And when she looked closer, her mouth went dry as she realized their faces were now mere inches apart. She hadn't realized she'd gotten quite that close. But she found she didn't want to move away. Not just yet.

Cabe's hand came up and covered hers, pressing her palm against his cheek. His skin was warm and slightly rough with a hint of stubble. Jason had always shaved twice daily, as he couldn't stand having a five-o'clock shadow. It didn't seem to bother Cabe, though. And she found his rough exterior... sexy. Her fingers itched to wander across those whiskers and explore more, but he was still looking at her in a way that made her go totally still.

Then his other hand came up and cupped her cheek, and she couldn't stop herself from leaning into his touch. The world around them seemed to shrink until it encompassed only her...and Cabe.

Her gaze went to his mouth, and she started to lean forward...

* * *

A sudden scream split the warm sensuality of the moment in two, and it took him a second to realize that Jessie was not only *not* kissing him, but that the scream hadn't come from her either.

She wheeled away from him in an instant, and Cabe's eyes scoured the area above them for the source of the cry. It came again, but this time ended in a shrill laugh.

Ah hell. It wasn't a distress cry. It was that first couple playing around as they ascended the rock.

When he glanced at Jessie, her eyes were also on the upper area of the dome, and when they came back down to meet his, she put the back of her hand over her mouth, a horror in her eyes that was worse than it should have been under the circumstances. Hell, it hadn't even been an actual kiss, so no harm no foul.

And if it had been?

And then, when she finally lowered her hand…she giggled.

What the…?

"Sorry," she said between gulped chortles. "I had no idea what that was. I thought someone was plummeting to their doom for a minute. And there we were in the middle of...well, who knows what that was."

He couldn't stop the smile that crept across his face. "I thought the same. I always have my climbing gear in the back of the car, just in case." Not that he could climb away from what had almost happened, as much as he might want to.

"Thank God it was a false alarm."

"Yes." What hadn't been a false alarm was how intent he'd been on her as she'd come closer, as she'd examined his wound. As her scent and warmth had surrounded him. So much so that he'd lost track of the world around him. Not good. This was a very public place. The last thing he needed was to see someone he knew and to have to explain why he'd been up here almost making out with the new vet. Only he hadn't been. And maybe she wouldn't have kissed him at all. Could be it was all in his damned imagination. He glanced over at Soldier to see he was still fast asleep. Yep. Not even that scream had woken him up. Maybe because in his subconscious he'd been able to tell the difference between what was real and what was not.

Kind of like Cabe was trying to do right now.

Well, what was very real was the fact that he didn't want to get carried away and end up in another relationship that had no business getting started. No matter how attractive he might find her.

He decided to prevaricate.

"Sometimes the beauty of the setting can kind of get the best of people. In a whole lot of ways."

"Evidently. I have no idea why I got so…" She shook her head. "This isn't, um, going to affect your participation in the community series, is it?"

He shook his head. "Why would it? If you think I'd pull out over a whole lot of nothing, I would say you don't know me very well, but in this case it's true. You don't know me."

If he'd been looking to drive home the fact that they were strangers, it seemed to have worked, because she scooted over to put some distance between them. "You're right. I don't. And I didn't come here to make friends, or anything else. I came here to do a job. And that's what I need to focus on right now. My work."

Why did he feel like he'd just made a mess out of something that he'd just called "a whole lot of nothing"? Maybe because that's what he did when it came to the opposite sex: made messes that were hard to clean up. But if he tried to backpedal, he might give her the wrong idea or make her think he was interested in anything she might have to offer. Well, she hadn't offered. And he wasn't interested. And it needed to stay that way. He knew what he could give someone. And he knew what he couldn't.

"I think that's something that we can both agree on. That our jobs are what are important to us—what we both need to focus on." He forced a smile. "So now that that's settled…"

Another screeched laugh came from somewhere above him and all of a sudden, he didn't want to sit here and listen to another couple's happiness. "Can I take you around to the lake side so you can see it?"

"Yes. Let's go."

* * *

He hadn't been kidding about needing to walk on water to see a display on this side. The road beside the Dome was narrow and there was nowhere to back up to in order to see a demonstration, until you were swimming offshore, and she didn't imagine anyone was going to want to come in their bathing suits.

Damn. What had almost happened? And there was no mistaking what she'd been about to do. It was as if she'd been mesmerized by him. After all the lectures about not leaping in and trusting another person...about it taking years before she felt safe enough to let her guard down. And here she was. Letting her guard down.

Well, up you go, Mr. Wall. Back in place.

She hadn't moved all the way to Santa Medina just to make the very same mistakes again. Yes, Cabe and Jason seemed very different. But that didn't mean that Cabe was any better for her than Jason had been.

So why had she almost done the unthinkable?

Like he'd said, maybe she'd been caught up in the scenery. Or seeing that first couple walking along in such unity. A unity she'd once dreamed of finding with her ex, only to have that dream turn into a nightmare. And something inside her now wondered if she was cut out for long-term relationships. If trust could ever truly be rebuilt.

"Which lake is this again?"

"Lake Tenaya."

She stared out at it, thankful for the stiff breeze that was not only whipping her ponytail around her face but also helping to blow away her troubling thoughts.

Jason was out of her life forever. And she needed to try to put the ugly things that had happened behind her.

Soldier sidled up next to her, and she reached down to pet his silky head, liking the way he leaned his weight against her hip. She wasn't quite ready to get another dog, but maybe that day was coming. He or she could never replace Chloe in her heart, but she knew the human heart was an amazing thing, able to carve out a new space and a different kind of love.

She glanced at Cabe.

Which was also why she needed to be on guard. While it might be okay for it to carve out a new spot for a companion animal, she didn't want it to think she was in the market for a new *human* companion.

"It's amazing." And it was. The sun glinted off the crystal-blue waters, mirroring the sky above. Both the lake and the sky were a beautiful contrast to the evergreens and rock formations that surrounded the area. A long sandy strip lay a short distance away, and there were several people sitting on the beach. "Do people swim here?"

"They do, but it's pretty chilly, even in late summer. Any other time, it's frigid."

"You're not a fan of polar plunge challenges?"

He smiled, his bandage crinkling slightly, which was what had gotten her into trouble before. She averted her eyes. "Let's just say, I'd choose my rock climbing over icy water any day."

"I would have to agree with you there. Even though I'm not crazy about heights, I think I might take your suggestion and find someplace to take lessons."

"I know a couple of good places. Or I could show you the basics."

He was willing to do that? Even after she'd

almost kissed him? It could be she was making a bigger deal about it than she needed to. He'd almost said as much.

But wouldn't being with him any more than necessary be playing with fire? Probably, but she was going to have to be with him for the seminar series. She could incorporate planning time into it and get a tiny glimpse into what search and rescue was all about.

"Are you sure? That would be great. It would be nice if I didn't go into your sessions having no clue as to what your team does. So can you talk me through a rescue as you show me those 'basics'?"

His gaze was on the lake, so she couldn't read his expression, but he seemed to have just tensed. Was he having second thoughts about his offer? Or just not thrilled about having to explain everything to her?

"We could just do one of the easy passes here on the Dome. I could show you how to use anchors and how to belay."

"Belay?" She gave an internal eye roll the second the question left her mouth. Case in point. Every time he mentioned something about climbing she sort of went *Huh?* But she wanted to learn. Wanted to know how the Santa Medina Search and Rescue team did what it did.

"Belay is a safety measure so you don't fall. It's why climbing in pairs is so important."

Her eyes widened. "Not falling would definitely be preferable to the alternative." She thought for a minute. "If you could show me some basics, I could decide if it's something I want to pursue further. With an actual instructor."

"They say some things are addictive. Rock climbing is definitely one of them."

She tensed. If anyone knew about addiction, it was her. And things about Jason made so much more sense now that she could look back on them. His single-minded pursuit of his sport. His seeming inability to get enough of her in bed while recovering from his shoulder injury. His secret drug use and subsequent denial that it was a problem. It seemed he could replace one addiction with another at will.

And Cabe's intensity about his work. Could it fall into that category? Somehow she didn't think so. But she had to admit, the man himself could be very, very addicting, if he put his mind to it.

She needed to be careful.

But what could it hurt to get a few pointers from the man? Maybe it would even help her understand more about the demonstration he and his team would put on in a few short weeks. If he even had time before then.

Soldier was following the edge of the lake, his nose to the ground like usual. She could see why Cabe loved him. The dog was very friendly and personable. Which was a testament to how well the paramedic treated him. And he was right about Soldier not limping anymore. If she hadn't treated him that day, she would have doubted anyone who told her the dog had been severely injured less than a week ago.

She re-found her train of thought. "Well, I don't know that I'll find rock climbing 'addictive,' but I'll certainly thank you for showing me a thing or two."

"Any other questions?"

A small part of her wished she had a million more questions. Because she had a feeling Cabe was bringing this trip to a close, and she found she wasn't quite ready for that.

Wasn't quite ready to leave the magic of this place behind.

But she couldn't stay here forever. Because this wasn't the real world. Or at least not her real world. So the sooner she could get that through her thick head, the better off she would be.

CHAPTER FIVE

HE WASN'T SURE why he'd come here today.

This was the first of Jessie's community seminars, and his participation didn't start until next week.

He'd told himself it was because he wanted to see how the format was laid out, so he kind of knew what to expect.

He sat in one of the plastic chairs in the waiting room area of the vet clinic, surprised by the fact that there were very few vacant seats. Maybe everyone else was as curious as he was about what these seminars were all about.

The trip to Tenaya Lake and the Dome had surprised him. Jessie had an easy way about her, from her curiosity about rock climbing to the effortless way she could keep a conversation alive. And better yet, she hadn't expected him to dive into any and every subject she brought up. He'd found it…restful.

And so different from his ex who'd expected him to weigh in on almost everything she said. It had been both exhausting and exasperating. And he knew part of that was his fault. He wasn't geared toward what he could only call chattiness. But he could have at least tried. The fact that he hadn't, was very telling. The weird thing was that her expectations after marriage had seemed very different from when they were dating in high school. But then again, their hormones had done a lot of the talking for both of them back then.

And then when talk of babies and children had started, he'd talked even less. Because he hadn't felt ready. Had still been dealing with some of the scars from his childhood and his father's drinking. Starting a family of their own terrified him. And he hadn't been able to find the words to tell her any of that, so he resorted to passively avoiding the subject, leaving Jackie to cajole and ask and finally to press the issue. Until he finally said, "Not right now." She'd gotten angrier than he'd ever seen her and replied, "Forget it. Having kids with you would be the biggest mistake of my life."

She'd moved out the next day.

Cabe had let her go without a fight. Mainly because he couldn't have agreed with her more. Having kids with him would be the biggest mistake of both of their lives. And in saying that, she'd done the job his father hadn't finished. Convinced him that he wasn't fit for the role of husband or father.

And yet he'd been willing to kiss Jessie, if their lips had connected that day on the Dome. Had sat there in full view of anyone passing by as if they were an ordinary couple.

They weren't.

So he wasn't sure why he'd offered to show her the basics of rock climbing. Or why he'd felt it important to show up at her clinic today.

Was it really just the curiosity? Hell, he hoped so.

Jessie was walking around the room, introducing herself to the people who'd showed up. Either she hadn't seen him yet, or she was purposely ignoring him. Her eyes hadn't made contact with his. Not even once.

And then she was on his row. In front of him. Holding her hand out, she waited for him to take it, just like she'd done with all the other strangers, before giving it a quick squeeze and releasing it. "Thanks for coming. Although you didn't have to."

"I wanted to see what to expect." He nodded at the front, where there were several kennels lined up. "I see they came prepared."

"Yes, I think they're hoping for a few adoptions today. Lillian is great, as is everyone I've met so far. She's going to talk about adopting out pets to companies who would like a mascot. She said it would be kind of modeled after a furniture store in Santa Medina that has a greeter dog. I haven't visited there yet, but I've heard it's a staple of their business. We never had anything like that in San Francisco, that I know of. Maybe because the city is so huge."

"Santa Medina Furniture. Yes, that would be Bosco. He's been there for years and is much loved by the owners and, I would dare to guess, by the store's patrons as well."

"It doesn't cause any problems?"

"Problems? Like what?"

"I don't know, allergies? People who don't like animals?"

"I don't think so. Most people here know what to expect when they go into those particular shops in town. And there's a sign in the door with Bosco's picture on it that says *Warning: Puppy Kisses Happen Here.* So even out-of-towners know what they're getting into if they go inside. Although Bosco is very well-behaved."

"Well, I certainly think that after meeting Soldier, there are dogs in shelters that could be trained as therapy or emotional support animals. Or maybe could even be used in a hospital or hospice setting as a source of comfort."

"I think that's a great idea."

One of the waitstaff from the local diner came over, reaching out to give Jessie a hug and thanking her for helping the shelter here in town. "I've taken in three dogs, but my husband has said no more. So I'm thrilled to see them getting some much-needed exposure."

"Of course. Every pet deserves a good home. And they're just as committed to making sure every would-be adopter gets the dog or cat that is perfect for them. I was pretty impressed with their vetting system."

Despite how new she was in town, she was obviously good at getting to know people, her natural warmth making them want to move into her circle of acquaintances. Including him.

Not only that, but her passion about finding homes for shelter dogs was obvious and it was hard not to get caught up in her enthusiasm. Her cheeks were flushed, and her eyes sparkled as she talked. Her high ponytail bobbled and swung, caressing her neck with each tilt of her head. The look suited her. Long and impossibly silky looking, it was hard not to imagine winding its length around his hand and...

Ah hell. There he went again.

The person moved away, and Jessie glanced up at the front where Lillian Crane was setting papers on a podium. "I think she's getting ready to start, so I'd better go introduce her."

"Okay."

He watched her walk up to the front of the room, hips twitching in a sinuous dance that was totally natural—and had none of the artifice that he'd seen in some other women.

Enough comparing, Cabe!

He got it. She was different. But that didn't mean it was going to change anything. He didn't want *anyone*. Didn't need anyone. And she certainly didn't need someone like him.

Jessie got through the introductions and then sat in the front row while Lillian gave a short speech on how the Santa Medina Animal Shelter was starting a campaign of making pets an integral part of the community and helping show their usefulness in the private, professional and the health-care sectors. That included business owners. Of course only *people* could adopt animals, not business entities themselves, so that pets would be cared for no matter what happened with a person's professional life. And the dogs that would be involved in public settings were to receive specialized training to make sure they had the qualities required and that they would actually enjoy interacting with people they didn't know.

Lillian rattled off eight businesses in the surrounding towns where companies had done just that. Taken the "bring your pet to work" idea to a whole new level, while raising community awareness. It also gave hope to dogs and cats that might languish in the shelter for months or even years. And it was catching on. After all, cat cafés were all the rage in some of the more urban settings. People went in for a coffee and the experience of having cats lounging around the shop or winding around their ankles. And the snapshots of daily adoptions that were sent across social media said that ankles weren't the only things those felines managed to wind around. For some, it was those same humans' hearts. More and more shelters were turning to inventive ways like this one to forge connections between people and pets.

Soldier was the closest thing Santa Medina Fire and Rescue had to a mascot, but since he was Cabe's pet, it wasn't quite the same thing. Maybe he should talk to Terry and see if that was something the department might think about doing.

Once she finished, Lillian proceeded to introduce different dogs to the audience, walking them around and letting people interact with them.

"Any one of these guys would be a welcome addition to a home or business. They're social and friendly and we did some training to measure temperament around people and children. They all passed with flying colors. They'd make wonderful companions or therapists. They're also good with other animals."

Thirty minutes later, Lillian was back at the front of the room, while people gathered around the four dogs she'd brought. He stood in the back and watched as one by one, each of the animals, with the exception of one, found a home. With good people. He knew each of them and had no doubt that the dogs were going to be well cared for.

The one dog that was left was a small fluffy-looking thing with wide-set eyes and a slightly crooked nose. When Lillian went to put her in her carrier, the dog looked around as if seeking someone…anyone.

Damn. He shouldn't go over there. He knew he shouldn't. He had no idea if Terry would even be open to the possibility of having a dog besides Soldier at the station house. But…

He went over and smiled. "Can I see him… her?…for a minute?"

"It's a her." She tilted her head. "I'm not sure Carrie is suited for search and rescue. She's kind of a couch potato."

Lillian put the dog into his arms and she immediately curled into them, tucking her nose into the crook of his elbow. "Not search and rescue, but maybe the squad would be willing to take on a mascot. I'm thinking her small size might be a good thing in this case. She's crate-trained?"

"Of course. And great with kids. She'd be good for all of those elementary school kids who come by on field trips."

"You don't have to sell me. You have to sell Terry."

"Terry's a cream puff. I'll call him my-self."

He gave her a crooked grin. "Any chance you can keep my name out of that conver-sation?"

"Um…no. So maybe you'd better bring it up before I make that call."

He stroked Carrie's silky ear. "Okay, I will. But I can't promise you anything."

"Hey, if you guys aren't smart enough to take her, I'm sure we'll find a good home for her. Her quirky features are pretty endearing, you have to admit."

Yes, he did. Which is why he needed to hand her back. But not before promising he'd do his best for her.

Lillian slipped her back into her crate. "Let me know, okay? Soon."

"I will."

As the audience members filtered out, he went to find Jessie. To what? To congratulate her? The seminar hadn't directly benefited her, from what he could see, but it had done both the community and those dogs a lot of good. Maybe even Carrie, if he could talk Terry into it.

He found her by the side door thanking people for coming. He got in line behind everyone else. When it was finally his turn he shook her hand yet again, smiling at how silly that custom seemed right now. "I'm impressed."

"Impressed?"

"Lillian came with four dogs and she's leaving with one. And I have hopes that maybe the station house will take her on."

She smiled. "That was kind of the idea behind the series."

"Finding homes for dogs?"

"No. Making animals a normal part of close-knit communities like Santa Medina. Maybe with enough education, there will be fewer dogs and cats that wind up in shelters. And those that do will have an easier time finding homes."

He got it. "Well, if today is anything to go by, then you're certainly on your way to doing that. Did you get any other organizations besides me lined up to participate?"

"Yep. As a matter of fact, I did. I have a farmer who's going to come in and talk about working dogs on farms, like Aussies and other breeds. And then I have a local school for developmental disabilities coming in to talk about service animals. The police department is trying to clear a date too."

"Well, it sounds like the seminars are going to be a success. And here you were worried about not having enough people to participate."

"I think I have you to thank, honestly."

"Me?" He had no idea how he could have anything to do with it.

"It got around that Santa Medina Search and Rescue was participating, and suddenly I started getting phone calls from other people wanting to know if I'd be interested in their organizations joining in."

"Well, I'm glad, although I had nothing personally to do with anyone finding out." If anything, he'd kind of kept it on the down low, but… "Maybe my boss had something to do with that."

"Whoever it was, I'm thankful."

Realizing there was someone behind him, he started to move out of the way before pausing. "About that rock climbing. Do you have time this next week? Before my seminar?"

"Let me look, and I'll give you a call."

Then she was greeting the woman behind him, and Cabe headed out the door, hoping that agreeing to give her a few pointers wasn't a huge mistake.

It would only be a mistake if he let it be one. If anything, this would give him the chance to work with Jessie and do a reset of their interactions. Putting that visit to the Dome firmly behind both of them. Where it needed to stay.

As long as he could remember that. No

more fantasies about that ponytail or any other part of the veterinarian.

The climbing vest felt like a foreign entity. Jessie found herself dressed in a mess of curling cords and clanging metal. It reminded her of Medusa. And as Jessie glanced up at the Dome, it suddenly seemed a whole lot more formidable than it had the last time they'd been here. This time Soldier hadn't accompanied them, and it made her wonder just how high Cabe was planning to go that he couldn't bring the dog with them. Maybe she should double-check.

"You do remember I've never done this before, right?"

"Yep. Don't worry, I'll take it easy on you. Nothing you can't handle."

He had a lot more confidence in her abilities than she did, evidently. "You have no idea what I can handle," she muttered.

"I guess we'll find out."

Great. She hadn't meant him to hear that last phrase but leave it to her to have an instructor who had super sensitive bat hearing.

He stepped over to her and clipped what

seemed like a hundred more carabiners onto the rings on her vest.

"Holy cow, am I going to need all of those?"

"No. But you always want more of them than you'll need. See?" He showed her his own harness.

"Heavens."

He pressed something into her hand. "This is a belay. We talked about this a little bit the other day. This is how it works."

He demonstrated how to feed the rope through the device hand over hand. "It's important to remember that your brake hand never ever leaves the brake side of the rope, which should always be on the bottom." He showed her one more time. "Now let me see you do it."

She felt like she had a thousand fingers—none of them very coordinated—as she practiced the counting and hand switching from the top to the bottom rope as she showed him. "Like this?"

"Yes. Try it again."

When she started to take her hand off the brake, he made a sound, and she stopped. "Right. Brake hand never let go. Got it."

They went through several other safety

features, and he showed her how to build in redundancies. "In the climbing world, redundancies are a good thing. They provide extra security in case something fails."

"Ugh. The last thing I want to think about when I'm up there is something failing."

He smiled and repeated, "Redundancies. They're good."

He also showed her how to load her carabiner in the right way so that her slings and cordelettes were always on the strongest side of the metal clasp.

Lordy. To show her half this stuff, meant he had to get close to her. So close, she could smell the light aftershave he wore. Could feel him loading things onto her body. And she got a close-up view of those tiny stubbles that had tempted her fingertips. The man was sexy beyond belief.

And now she was going to climb the Dome. With him.

Well, at least an easier part of it.

"So we're going to head up to the first anchor bolt and I'm going to show you how to tie off and how to belay."

"You don't really expect me to stop you from falling, do you?"

"I do."

The matter-of-fact words made her shiver. "And you'll keep me from falling?"

"I will."

The solemness of his words made her wonder if they were talking about falling as in mountain climbing, or some other kind of falling.

And maybe they were. Because over the last couple of days, she could see how it might be possible to fall for this man. And she did not want to. Heavens, she so did not want to.

She'd just gotten out of a relationship that at one time she'd thought was wonderful. It turned out it wasn't. At all. She did not want to jump back into another one that would either end in the same way…or worse. She liked Cabe. She didn't want to ruin things by developing some kind of crush on the man. It was okay to find him attractive. And she did. Very much so. But what was not okay was to think of him in terms of a romantic partner.

Especially not when she was just establishing herself in this community. She'd seen how her community seminar program had grown once it became known that Cabe was participating. If they had some kind of falling-out, it could have the opposite effect. She needed to get established in Santa Medina on her own terms and because of her own skills rather than riding on someone else's coattails.

That wouldn't be fair to Cabe. And it wouldn't be good for her.

"Okay, ready? I'm going to go up to the first point, while you work the belay."

A quick thrill of fear went through her. "Are you sure, Cabe? What if I drop you?"

"You won't. And even if you get confused, it's a short climb, and I'll have a good grip. Okay. On belay?"

She checked everything and then repeated the response he'd taught her, signaling she was prepared. "Belay on."

As he headed up, she kept the slack at a minimum while he was actively climbing. And then when he stopped, he asked her to let him have more.

"Okay, I have the anchor and sling set up up here. Rope?"

"Okay."

He threw the length of rope down to her, while she fumbled around with it to get it where it needed to be. Oh, God, she couldn't believe she was about to do this, even though it looked pretty much like she could walk up it without needing the rope. But beneath the fear was a slight tingle of excitement. Very slight. But it was there nonetheless.

He gave her instructions each step of the way. And with each footfall that successfully landed on solid rock, that tingle of excitement grew, until she was within an arm's length of him. He held his hand out and the second hers connected with his, the warmth of his palm set off a series of tiny explosions as he pulled her the few remaining feet. She stood there staring at him, breath sawing in and out of her lungs until he finally turned away and showed her how to clip herself to the locking carabiner he'd set up. Then they were both tethered to the rock on hooks that looked like a tiny pop tab from a soda can. The fear came creeping back. "Are you sure that's going to hold both of us?"

"Positive. They're drilled deep into the rock. It can hold a couple thousand pounds each. Just lean back against your harness. It'll help you rest your muscles."

She gingerly did as he suggested and found

that it actually didn't feel as scary now that she was up here as she'd expected it to. She glanced up at the clear blue of the sky above her. It seemed so much closer than it did from the ground, although she knew that was her imagination. But still. "Whew. My mom will never believe that I did this."

"Really? Why not?"

Jessie laughed, her gaze settling back on him. "Because neither of us like heights."

"We're not that high up. But the key when you're climbing is to keep looking up. Just take one anchor bolt at a time and always be looking for the next one."

"So what you're saying is never look down." Almost as soon as she said it, the urge was there to do exactly that.

As if he knew, he leaned closer. "Don't do it."

She pulled in a deep breath, seeing wisps of his dark hair as they blew across his forehead. She resisted the urge to brush them back..

He glanced at her. "So what do you want to do now? Ascend to the next bolt? Or head back down?"

She thought for several seconds, remembering how thrilling making it up this first section had been. "Is it exactly the same process?"

"Exactly. It's constant repetition. Until it all becomes muscle memory."

Constant repetition. Muscle memory. Was it really that easy? "Okay. One more."

In the end, they climbed to three anchor bolts before her leg muscles started screaming in protest. And she still hadn't looked down. That had to be something, didn't it? Part of conquering that fear?

She leaned against her harness to catch her breath. "This is hard work. Really hard work. But it feels good too." She could see where he got his muscles. Even now, the bulges in his biceps were obvious, and she'd bet his legs had the same corded muscle as his arms. She knew for a fact that his glutes were well defined. She'd seen the evidence firsthand. She smiled at the memory.

"What?"

"Nothing."

His head tilted, but he didn't try to press her for an answer. Instead, he said, "Okay, if you want to look out over the view, now is the time."

Her brain seized for a second at the thought. "You mean it's okay to look down?"

"Yep. Once you reach your goal, it's okay to look."

Taking a deep breath, she turned her head to look and a sense of wonder came over her. God, it was stunning. All of it. Including him. "I'm at a loss for words." She made herself pull phrases out of thin air. "It—it's staggeringly beautiful."

They were higher up than she thought they were going to be. And really, Cabe had done most of the work as the lead climber, but the exhilaration that came over her as she gazed across the scenery threatened to overwhelm her. "Now I get it, Cabe."

"Do you?" His blue eyes were focused on her face, and it caused the tingle from earlier to spread, sliding over in her midsection and beyond before pinging back and lodging in her heart.

"Yes. I do."

His fingers reached out and traced across her cheek. "I think you do."

Then his touch was gone, and he was no longer smiling. Instead a muscle worked in his cheek, and strange longing built in the pit of her stomach.

Not good.

Before she had time to dwell on it, he was reviewing the steps to get back down again. They would do what was called short roping, where they would be attached to each other with a short rope, and he would follow her down since the slope wasn't that steep. "I'm going to undo our anchors, and then we'll go."

Once he had everything stowed away on his harness, he told her to go in front and she walked down the way he had showed her earlier, praying she didn't trip over her own two feet. She didn't, and they made it back down to their starting point a lot more quickly than it had taken them to go up. Thank God. There was something cathartic about having conquered one of her fears. But she was also very glad she was back in control of her own movements. Something about having Caleb direct her steps had made her feel vulnerable in a way she hadn't felt in a long time. And she wasn't sure she liked it.

When they were on the ground, he detached the rope. "And now you can say you've rock climbed the Stately Pleasure Dome."

"Well, at least a tiny part of it." She smiled. "Seriously, thank you so much, Cabe. I can honestly say that wasn't even on my bucket list of things to do, but it should have been. I actually think I might take classes. I'd like to try to do one of the easier climbs."

"I think you'll make it." He scribbled something down on a piece of paper he had in his vest. "Here. This is the name of someone I trust. He'll get you up there safely."

A tingle of disappointment went through her that he hadn't offered to teach her, but then again, he'd told her he was willing to show her the basics but had never promised anything more than that. Why not just be glad that he'd helped her see rock climbing through different eyes?

Yes. She would do exactly that. "Thank you again. Hopefully I'll never need SAR as I'm learning."

"I think you're going to do just fine."

"Hey!" A frantic voice called from above them. "We need help! Injured climber at the top of the Dome."

It was like the scream they'd heard the last time they visited the Dome. Only this time, no one was laughing.

CHAPTER SIX

THE MAN WAS climbing down the Dome.

"Go back up and wait. I'll be right there!"

Cabe turned to Jessie. "I need you to call Doug or Brad over at the SAR office and get them over here. They're both paramedics." He threw the number at her and waited until she'd punched it in.

He was going to need to self-belay to the top. As a beginner, there was no way that Jessie could follow him up. Besides, this was one of the more challenging climbs. He didn't have his medical gear with him, but Doug or Brad would be bringing that.

He did a quick check of his gear, making sure he was ready and then went into rescue mode, starting up the Dome.

"Good luck, Cabe!"

Unable to answer at the moment, all he could do was climb. And climb.

It seemed like forever until he reached the peak of the Dome, and his breathing was the deep gasps that came with heavy exertion. The man that had called down met him. "A little dog tried to follow us up the Dome and got in trouble. When my wife tried to help it, she fell. The rope caught her, but she's not answering when I call to her."

The man motioned to the side and sure enough a little white ball of fluff was crouched on the edge of the cliff, shivering. Damn. How on earth had it made it up this far?

Leaning against his harness, he called Jessie's cell phone. She answered on the first ring. "Are you okay?"

"Fine. There's a dog in trouble up here. If we can get him or her lowered down, can you take it?"

"Absolutely. Tell me where and when."

"I'm handing you off to another climber." He glanced at another man in the group. "Can you get him in your pack without getting injured? There's a vet on the ground."

"Yes. I'll meet her partway down."

"She's a novice."

"Got it."

Cabe handed over the phone and turned his attention back to the situation at hand. He peered over the side and saw a woman hanging from one of the outcroppings. The wind was stronger up here and kept blowing her back to the rock, periodically knocking her into it. She was unconscious. "Did she just lose her balance?"

It only made a difference in that it would let him know if there was equipment failure or she'd simply moved the wrong way and slipped.

"Her foot slipped on some loose rocks…" The man's voice caught, the anguish on his face evident. "We have a little girl at home. If something happens to her, I'll never forgive myself."

"We'll get her down." Just then his cell phone went off and the other man handed it back to Cabe. "McBride here."

"Cabe, it's Doug. What have you got?"

He quickly relayed what he knew so far, before saying, "I'm going to head down. She's swinging from the southeast face. I don't have enough rope to lower her from there, but…" He turned to the woman's companion. "How much rope do you have?"

"I have enough."

"Good. Give it to me."

The man handed over a heavy coiled rope. Out of the corner of his eye, he saw the second man picking up the dog, who offered no resistance. He tucked the animal into his vest. Then he put his own phone to his ear giving some logistics. He must be talking to Jessie. Good.

"What's your wife's name?"

"Gloria. I'm Jerry, her husband. I—I didn't dare try to lower her myself."

Cabe was glad he hadn't. "You did the right thing. Wait here until I tell you it's safe to descend." The last thing he needed was someone to follow him down and get tangled up in his gear or go all emotional on him. This was where Cabe excelled. The lack of emotion in his marriage that had ultimately destroyed it, served him well in SAR. He could make decisions based on true objectivity rather than putting himself in someone else's shoes and imagining what they were going through.

"Doug, you still there?"

"Yep. I'm around on that side now. I see her."

"Good. I'm going to set up belay on the rope her partner gave me, and you can use that to lower her once she's clipped in."

"Got it. I'll be ready. I saw Jessie. She said someone's bringing down a dog? From up there?"

"Yep."

He couldn't see Doug because of the outcropping, but that didn't matter. He would have to hope he could catch the bottom part of Gloria's rope and pull her in long enough to get the longer rope hooked to her harness. If he knew Doug, the squad was already en route.

Painstakingly making his way to the outcropping, he anchored himself in and then laid out flat along it to look at the conditions. She was about ten feet below him, still free-swinging, still no signs of consciousness. "Gloria? Can you hear me?"

His call got no response the first time. He tried again.

This time he heard a loud groan, but she didn't move. There was blood on her temple and on the shoulder of her climbing harness.

He was right. She had some kind of head injury, which meant they needed to get her down as soon as possible. He looked up the way he'd come at her companion.

"Jerry, I'm going to finish making my way down to her. It looks like she hit her head. The plan is to lower her down with my partner on belay."

"Okay."

Cabe found a good bolt and anchored to it, then went over the side of the outcropping, feeling for toe and finger holds until he got to a more vertical section of rock, and thankfully found another bolt. The trick now would be to guide her close enough to clip her and hook her in above, while Doug guided her down, hopefully without her hitting the sheer wall any more than necessary.

The wind blew the loose end of her rope toward him, and he caught it on the first try. Rechecking his attachment point, he threaded her rope through one of the relays and using it as a pulley, guided her close enough for him to reach. Once he'd secured her to the master anchor, he checked her over as quickly as he dared. She was breathing and pupils were equal, thank God.

Satisfied she wouldn't swing back out again, he put Doug on speaker. "I've got her hooked into me. I'm going to throw you the excess rope."

"Go."

Taking a good swing that he hoped would clear all of the jutting rocks, he tossed the rope into space. He clipped his phone to his vest, leaving the line open.

"Got it, Cabe. Setting up belay."

Five minutes later, his partner's voice came back through. "Ready when you are. The squad is here."

"Good news."

With each of them working on opposite ends, Cabe fed his rope through his carabiner to slowly lower the injured woman, while Doug kept the line taut and stable and guided the path of the descent. For five nerve-racking minutes there was silence over the line, other than the grunts of exertion as Doug worked to keep the pressure exactly where it needed to be.

"She's down, I've got her!"

Cabe's rope went slack along with what seemed like every one of his muscles. He clung to the rock for several minutes, knowing he wouldn't be able to descend fast enough to help with her care. And he needed to rest, or his own descent wasn't going to be pretty. He called up. "Jerry, she's down. Do you have enough rope to get yourself down?"

"Yes. God! Thank you! We were so lucky you were here. I'm heading down. Lloyd just texted that he got the dog down to your wife, too."

Wife? Oh, hell, no. But then he hadn't recognized any of the trio, so there was no way they could have known that he and Jessie weren't related. But it still made his gut twist in a way that said the words had hit a nerve. And to try to explain it to Jerry? Not going to do it.

So all he said was, "Safe climbing."

With that he let himself lean his weight against his harness. Now that the crisis was over—at least his part of it—his adrenaline seeped away in a rush, along with any reserve energy he might have had left. But he couldn't hang here forever, and he needed to get back down in case the dog was in bad shape, and he needed to drive them back to the clinic. Or maybe she'd already gone. So he began the painstaking process of heading down the Dome on one of the more challenging tracts. But it was either that or climbing back over the summit and then going down the other side. In the spots he could, he bounced off the face of the Dome and could go quickly. Where it was too treacherous, he locked himself in and toed his way down. And then his feet hit solid ground and he stood there for a minute pulling down deep breaths.

Suddenly he felt a hand grip his, and when he looked, Jessie was there, her face pale. The white dog was tucked under her arm. Was it in worse shape than he thought?

"Is he all right?"

She opened her mouth several times to speak and finally she said. "Yes. *She's* fine. No injuries that I could find. But please, *please* tell me that's not what the demonstration is going to look like. I was paralyzed the whole time you were up there."

Hell, she *sounded* like a wife.

All of a sudden, Cabe laughed. Big bellowing laughs that were much larger than the situation warranted, but the relief of getting Gloria down hit him all at once, and he found himself turning and enveloping her in a big hug that went on and on and on.

From the region of his chest, her muffled voice came back to him. "They think she's got a mild concussion, but they're obviously taking her in to be sure there isn't anything more serious going on."

"And Jerry, her husband?"

"He made it down, and he's in the ambulance with her." She leaned back to look up at him. "He's very grateful. And so am I, for…" She nodded toward the tiny bundle tucked against her body. Suddenly her lower lip trembled, and a tear slid down her cheek.

He got it. He really did. He always imagined the rescues looked worse from the ground than they did from his perspective on the rock. Although this one was pretty hairy.

He caught the tear with his thumb. "Hey it's okay. We all made it. Including your tiny charge."

"I know but…*whew*!" She gave a shaky smile. "Maybe I'll hold off on those lessons."

He slung his arm around her shoulder, unsure if it was because he needed the stability or if he just needed to be close to another human being right now, and they headed back to the car.

"Come back to my place?" she said. "I'll get you some tea and something to eat. From the feel of her, Rocky needs some food too."

"Rocky?"

"It's what I'm naming her for now. At least until I can look for her owner. Hopefully someone will claim her."

"Rocky fits her, considering where she was found." He was grateful she hadn't offered him alcohol. Although he wasn't sure why he thought she would. "Anyway, I accept on both counts."

Jessie's knees were still knocking by the time they made it back to her place. What she'd witnessed had been both thrilling and terrifying. And it had shaken her to her core. Cabe and Gloria could have both plummeted to their death and the thought of that…

He'd looked done in too, and who could blame him. He'd done all the work. If they hadn't been there, how long would it have taken for help to get there? Sure, Doug had gotten there within about fifteen minutes, but Cabe was already almost at the top by the time he arrived.

She directed him to the sofa and urged him to sit down.

"I'm fine," he said.

Dumble evidently had to get his two cents' worth in, because he started in immediately. "Not the only one. Not the only one."

He'd been repeating that phrase almost nonstop for the last week, and she had no idea where it had come from. When he caught sight of the dog, he gave his whistle and said, "Good doggy."

When she turned to glance at Cabe he was making a face at the bird. "Sorry. I know he's annoying."

"No, he's fine."

"I'll be right back. I'm going to give Rocky something to eat and drink."

Once she set two bowls on the floor, the dog immediately drank. So far she seemed perfectly fine, settling in to eat the food.

Going back into the living room to ask Cabe what he wanted to eat, she glanced at him. "Oh! Your butterflies have come off."

It was almost a week, but evidently the

sweat and exertion had decided to do the rest of the job.

Moving closer, she examined the dirt-streaked skin, surprised when he didn't try to brush her away. "It looks good. I think it'll do."

Warm fingers curled around the nape of her neck. "Thanks for sticking around."

"Where else would I be?"

"You could have left."

A sense of mirth went through her. "You took the car keys with you. I'd have had to hot-wire your car, something else I know nothing about."

His thumb took a slow, treacherous course, moving from just behind her ear all the way down her neck. "Is that the only reason why you stuck around?"

"No," she whispered, realizing it was true. Nothing could have dragged her from that dome while he was up there fighting for someone's life. It had moved her in a way she didn't understand. Didn't want to examine.

Before she had time to analyze her thoughts anymore, his lips came up and caught hers, pressing tiny kisses all along her bottom lip, before sucking it into his mouth. The sensation sent fiery signals along her nerve endings, obliterating everything in their path.

The shock of seeing that rescue unfold in living color and the reality that he could have been killed at any point during it still hung in the foggy areas of her mind. She'd been so scared. And then after the woman was lowered and whisked away, Cabe had hung out on those jagged rocks for several minutes not moving. She'd thought at first he'd been hurt too, distracting her as she looked Rocky over for injuries. The relief when he finally started moving down had held her transfixed at the base of the Dome. It held her transfixed even now, as his kisses started reawakening parts of her body that had been sleeping for a while. Until that first trip to the Dome.

And until now.

She thought she'd succeeded in putting those feelings to bed. Or maybe bed was what it was going to take to squash out those embers. If so, she was all in.

It was Sunday, and she was off for the rest of the day. That suddenly seemed like a huge luxury. And to spend it with this man…

She shifted on the couch, straddling his hips in a way that said she'd be satisfied with nothing less than full contact. The Full Monty. She wanted her hands on the butt she had glimpsed that first day at the clinic. In reality it had teased at her every time she'd seen him since then. Every time she'd spent time with him. Maybe it had been leading up to this the whole time.

And maybe this was what it would take for her to stop feeling that sense of yearning.

Vaguely she became aware of strange sounds coming from behind her, but since Cabe's lips had pushed aside the V-neck of her shirt and were now getting tantalizingly close to areas that were screaming for his attention, she tuned it out. Until he stopped.

God! He wasn't going to leave, was he?

She leaned back to look at him. "What is it?"

He nodded at something behind her. "It's him." She twisted around and heard the sound again. She realized it was Dumble. He was staring at them, his head twisting this way, then that, making the most obnoxious kissing sounds known to man.

She swallowed, then slowly turned back to Cabe. Jason had hated it when the bird taunted him. Had gotten truly angry about it at times.

But Cabe didn't look angry. He was smiling.

"I'm really not up for a threesome today." Then Rocky appeared at the base of the couch. "Make that a foursome. You wouldn't happen to have a bedroom in this place, would you?"

"As a matter of fact, it's right down that hallway. And it has a door that can be closed. Let me just barricade her in the kitchen." Jessie scooped the puppy up, a sense of euphoria taking over as she put Rocky in the kitchen while Cabe came over and tipped her small dinette table on its side and put it in front of the door.

Then he turned to her and put his arms under her butt, scooping her up so fast that she squealed, having to wrap her calves around his back to keep her balance. Well, she guessed she didn't have to ask if he'd changed his mind. He evidently hadn't. And neither had she.

"It's down the hall, first door on your right."

Every step he took was torture; the rhythmic press and release against the most sensitive part of her seemed geared toward driving her crazy.

And it was working.

Dumble and Rocky were left behind as Cabe slid into her bedroom and closed the door by leaning against it. Then he kissed her on the lips, seeming in no hurry to move from this spot. Fortunately, he had taken his climbing vest off before getting into the car, so he was left with just a long-sleeved T-shirt.

While he continued to kiss her, she bunched the shirt in her hands and tugged it upward, but her thighs were pinning it in place. She squirmed, but still couldn't pull it free.

His lips went still. "Need some help?"

"Yes."

He started walking toward her bed and then leaned over it and let go of her, bracing his arms on the mattress. The sudden lack of support made her fall onto the soft surface.

He chuckled, then went onto his elbows and kissed her nipple through her own T-shirt and bra. The sudden contact made her arch against him, eyes closing as she moaned.

And then he was gone.

Her eyes sprang back open and found him hauling his shirt up his taut stomach and pulling it over his head. It went onto the floor.

She sat up and started to do the same, only to have him stop her. "That's my job."

Warm hands slid her shirt up her torso, taking their time when he reached the curves of her breasts. And then her shirt too was gone. Whisked away and dropped on top of his. The juxtaposition of her clothes on top of his seemed to carry a weird intimacy. She pulled her glance away from it before she read more into it than she should.

Lean hips met her view, and her hands couldn't resist sliding around them until she found his jeans-covered butt. "You should have worn your other pants."

"My other...?"

She slid her fingers into his back pocket. "Hmmm...it would have made things so much easier."

He caught her meaning and laughed. "Those jeans didn't survive their ordeal."

Her calves slid around his and held him

in place. "It's okay. I think we can figure something out."

Her fingertips skimmed around the bare skin of his waist, taking in the changes in topography formed by the different muscle groups. This man was certainly not soft. Her eyes settled on the area behind his zipper— definitely not soft.

She popped the button on his jeans free and then slowly slid the fastener down, hearing a hissed breath from above her when she purposely put more pressure than necessary on what was behind that zipper.

Pushing his jeans and briefs down his thighs, she reached behind him and squeezed his glutes, her eyes closing as she acted on the fantasy she'd had for the last week. God, they didn't disappoint. That soft layer of skin was stretched tight over muscles that were unbelievably hard. That rippled beneath her touch.

Just like what was right in front of her face. Hard and warm, and jerking with a need that she could definitely understand.

The hands on his ass reeled him in until she could just…

Slide over him.

The groaning sound from above her was all the affirmation she needed to know that he liked what she was doing. A lot. As did the gentle pull against her scalp that said he must have her ponytail bunched in his hand, the way she'd done with his shirt. The mental picture was almost too much, ramping her need up higher than it had ever been. But when she slid her tongue slowly along his length, that same grip on her hair was used to ease her free.

When she looked up, his eyes were clamped shut, a muscle working frantically in his jaw before slowing.

Then he looked at her, and his gaze was molten silver, scorching over her before his hands settled on her shoulders. With a single push, she fell back onto the mattress, and he shed the rest of his clothes, pulling something from his wallet before he leaned down, settling his elbows on either side of her head.

"Not fair," he muttered against her mouth. "So not fair."

She smiled her response. Oh, it was plenty fair. And fun. And incredibly hot.

What he lacked in the area of communication, he made up for in things that didn't require a whole lot of talking. And she found she liked it. Liked using the reactions of his body as a guide for what he liked.

And so far, he'd liked pretty much all of it. A lot.

So had she.

He sheathed himself. But where she expected him to just hunch down over her and drive himself home, he didn't. Not that that would have been a bad thing. It wouldn't have. She was ready.

But evidently, he wasn't.

Reaching behind her, he unclasped her bra and tugged it free of her body, tossing it behind her. Then she felt him move between her legs, before standing up completely.

"No!"

"Shh... I'm not leaving. Not a chance."

His hands covered her breasts, kneading them with a gentle motion that was unbelievably erotic before moving on to her hips and then lower.

That first touch was electric, and she arched up with a low moan as his thumb stroked over her, moving in time with the rhythm her hips set up. Soon it wasn't enough. She needed more. So much more.

Her arms reached for him, as the point of no return became visible...unavoidable. "Cabe...please." The words carried a quiet desperation that she hoped he caught.

He did.

He was there in a flash, muscles bunching in his arms as his hands lifted her hips off the mattress, so he could drive home in one stroke. Then she was full. So unbelievably full, as he moved inside her. It was an ecstasy she'd never experienced. With anyone.

There'd always been too much talking. Too many questions about what she liked, what she didn't. This was what she liked. Being able to concentrate on how he made her *feel*.

And it was...overpowering. Overwhelming. Just like seeing him on that mountain had been. This time she didn't need carabiners. Didn't need belay devices. She just needed him, ratcheting her higher and higher with each stroke of his body.

She was right. This was what she needed to do away with that awful tension that had been building inside her ever since she met him.

Her legs pinned him against her even as he continued to move, continued to tighten the gears. As he held her up with one hand, his other returned to stroke her, making her hips jerk against him. As her need increased, so did her speed. It didn't matter what he was doing at this point, because she could only focus on that peak of the mountain that was so close. So so close. So...

Then she shot past it, sailing out into open air as her body spasmed around him. On some level she was aware of his shouted cry above her, of his hands gripping her hips, of his movements that came at lightning speed before slowing. Her own body slowed as well, as she floated down, eyes closing as she tried to hang on to those few last seconds of dreamy sensation before they were gone.

She drew in a deep breath, one arm curling around her head as she tried to regather her senses. Then he slid free, and she frowned.

"Sorry. My phone is buzzing."

Her ears picked up the sound coming from somewhere beside the bed.

Well, at least he wasn't lying to get out of there.

Although maybe he should have.

She sat up in a rush. What had just happened here? Yesterday, she'd been thinking of all the reasons she didn't want to get involved with anyone. Of how little she even knew about Cabe.

Of how hard it was going to be to trust again.

Of course you didn't need to trust someone to have sex. Right?

She might have agreed with that argument a few minutes ago, but right now she wasn't so sure. Because sex could lead to caring.

And she didn't want to care.

Not right now. Maybe not ever.

God…she was so confused. So… She felt like she was the one stuck on that mountain, dangling in space, trying to gather enough strength to get herself down in one piece.

And she couldn't do that if she let herself get emotionally involved all over again.

So while he pulled on his clothes, she pulled herself together and dragged the bedspread around her body, so that she felt at least a little less vulnerable.

Then she forced herself to look at him, even as he finished his call and shoved his feet into his shoes. "Hey, this can't change anything between us, okay? This was just good clean fun that—" she forced herself to use his words from the other day when she'd almost kissed him "—that was a whole lot of nothing."

"Of course."

The words came fast. Too fast. With a sense of relief that was unmistakable.

She should have felt a relief of her own, but instead there was just a quiet sense of unease as if her brave-sounding words were just that. Words. Words, that, like her proclamation, meant nothing.

She might be able to say that what they'd done had changed nothing, but she had a feeling it was all a lie.

That what they'd done had changed things in ways that she couldn't yet understand.

But she had a feeling it would become all too clear as time went on.

So all she could do was hold off the inevitable for as long as possible, and hope that whatever changes today had made could be undone.

Which meant, she couldn't sleep with him again. And while she wasn't going to say that to him directly, as he gave a quick good-bye salute and left her room, as he walked past Dumble who made more obnoxiously loud kissing sounds, she was going to make it very clear by *her* actions, that no further action was required on his part. Then she fell back onto the bed and tried to make herself believe it.

CHAPTER SEVEN

HE HADN'T HEARD from her in almost a week. And as he sat with the guys at the squad house and ate the chili someone had thrown together for lunch, he wondered why that surprised him. It shouldn't. But his part in her seminar series was coming up in two days. Maybe she'd decided to kick him off the schedule. Not that he could blame her.

The last thing he'd expected when he came down off that mountain was to feel what he had as he'd leaned his weight on her as they'd walked to the car. He'd felt a sense of companionship. A sense of belonging that was alien to him.

But that probably had more to do with the way Jessie made people feel than it did with actually belonging in her circle. She had a way about her that was warm and inviting and made those around her feel special.

He'd fallen for that spell. Until after they'd had sex, and *she'd* been the one to say the words that he should have said. But hadn't.

And he wasn't even sure why.

Letting himself believe in fairy tales would be a big mistake, even if she hadn't made it clear that the sex had been as meaningless as the handshakes she'd given to him at that first seminar.

But he wasn't sure it had been as meaningless to him. And that bothered him on an elemental level. He'd never had a hard time separating his personal life from his professional, but now he found that thoughts of Jessie were encroaching even in the very spaces he held sacred.

Doug's voice came across the table at him. "You sure you're okay? You've seemed on edge ever since you got called in on Sunday."

In the back of his head, he heard Jessie's bird making those lip-smacking sounds. If he wasn't careful, Dumble wouldn't be the only one making those noises at him. His squad buddies would too.

"I'm fine."

"Whatever you say, bro." Doug grinned at him in a way that said he wasn't buying whatever Cabe was shoveling. "Which reminds me. We probably need to practice for our demo in a couple of weeks. We need to get the timing down."

Since Cabe had had no idea if they were still in the lineup, all he could do was say, "Sure. Whenever you guys are ready."

They'd figured out that Brad and Doug would be helping with the demo. Cabe would be their lead climber, since they needed Soldier to alert to Brad, who would be hiding in one of the outcroppings of evergreens at one of the spots on the Dome. Brad would follow him up as the second person on the climbing team and work the brake. They wanted to be able to accomplish the mock rescue in a half hour, so the observers weren't standing around long enough to get restless or bored, which meant they needed to coordinate things almost down to the minute.

Brad spoke up. "Do you want to shoot for tomorrow?"

Perfect. So he needed to decide whether or not to call and talk to Jessie to make sure she hadn't changed her mind. Or he needed to just let things ride and hope for the best. Maybe he could show up on Saturday for the first part of his three sessions as if nothing had happened. She'd said it changed nothing, right? So maybe he should just take her at her word. They were both professionals. They could both handle working together these three times.

Then that would be that. He'd go back to his yearly vaccination schedules with Soldier, just like he'd planned back when she'd helped put his dog back together again. He fingered the spot on his cheek that she had patched. So far it had held.

Whatever had happened between them—whatever he'd had to patch back together again—would hold too. He'd make sure of it.

"Yes, let's shoot for tomorrow." Like Dumble, it seemed like all he could do was parrot his friend's words back to him. Well, he needed to shake himself out of his funk, before someone really took notice. And started to dig for the reasons behind it. He honestly didn't care if someone figured out he'd slept with someone. But Jessie might. And that mattered to him a whole lot more than it should.

So he would just keep on pushing forward and do his best to keep what had happened under wraps. Until it all blew over. Or until the butterfly bandages he'd slapped over those tricky emotional areas fell off of their own accord.

The calf wasn't budging.

The thing about being a vet in a rural town was that sometimes the calls were a whole lot different than they were in the city. Fortunately when she'd gone through vet school, she'd shot for a mixed practice degree—which encompassed both small and large animals—never expecting to use her large animal vet skills in San Francisco. But she'd hoped someday she'd be able to do both. So when Doc Humphrey's job request had come through, she'd been able to honestly say that she had expertise in both areas. And now, here she was. Under a cow. Trying to get her baby out of her.

If she could just reach one of its tiny front legs…

The owner was up by the heifer's head with a lead rope, to help keep everyone safe. When the call came through, Farmer Jonas said he'd woken up to the cow covered in sweat and straining. It was obvious she'd been working for a while. If Jessie could help it, she didn't want to hook a calf puller to it unless there was no other choice.

Which was why she was lying spread-eagled on the ground with her hand searching for those elusive legs. Without them moved into position, the baby's head wouldn't have enough room to be born.

Found one!

Just as quickly, the leg slipped from her grasp, and she had to start all over again. Feeling the head and following it down, down, down, until she felt...a leg! Using all her force she pulled it up next to the head and then reached for the second one. There!

The muscles in her arm were cramping from the effort and she could understand why Cabe had seemed so drained after rescuing that woman off the mountain.

Cabe. No thinking about him right now.

She'd pretty much chanted that to herself every time he came to mind. Sometimes her brain listened and sometimes it didn't. Like when she was asleep and couldn't fight against it any longer. Then the time in her bedroom played back through her dreams in stunning detail, causing her to wake up drenched in sweat.

Just like the heifer that she should be concentrating on. Forcing Cabe once again to move away, she hauled the baby's second leg up and lodged it beside the first.

Now she just had to hope the cow had enough left in her to push. Jasmine wasn't just a milk cow and a valuable asset to a family farm, she was also a pet, the farmer's kids finally convincing him that they should be allowed to name her. The rest was history. This baby was going to be her last, then when the baby was weaned, and her milk dried up, she would be retired to live out her days as a beloved family pet in a green pasture.

If Jessie could just get one more push out of the girl.

She slid her arm free. "Okay, Jasmine, come on, you can do it." She glanced up at the farmer, who'd sent his kids away once he realized the cow was in trouble. "I've gotten the front legs forward. Hold her while I give her a dose of oxytocin to stimulate her contractions."

Fortunately the hormone could be administered through the muscle, so she quickly pulled out the preprepared syringe and injected it. Jasmine was so tired, she didn't even flinch. Not a good sign.

"Come on, girl. Show us what you've got."

Another minute went by. Then two. And then...

A push. A good one.

It was followed by another, and finally she saw those two tiny feet emerge, exactly as they should have when this whole process had started hours ago. She glanced at her watch. An hour had gone by since she'd arrived on-site. Hopefully for both mom and calf, she hadn't been too late.

There! The head. "Almost there, Jazzy."

"That's what my kids call her."

The farmer's voice pulled her from her trance. She smiled over at him. "She looks like a Jazzy."

The shoulders emerged as Jessie focused on the baby's open eye, which she could just see through the sac, willing it to...

Blink! It blinked! Yes! She'd hoped they'd be able to at least save the heifer, but the fact that the baby was still viable...

One more push and the tiny creature was delivered.

As if energized by the birth of her calf, Jasmine came up sternal, reaching around to start cleaning her baby.

As long as she could do the rest herself, and the baby wasn't in trouble, Jessie was okay letting her bond with the gal. "You've got yourself a new little heifer."

"Good. Now if I can just keep my kids from naming this one too." He removed the lead rope from the cow and let her stand to finish the job, while Jessie cleaned up and put away her gear. She needed to wait for the placenta to emerge and for the baby to get to her feet. But it looked like this might be one lucky mama and baby.

"I think it's safe to call the kids back out here."

"Thank God. I had no idea how I was going to explain it to them if one or both of them died."

He used his phone to call the house and within seconds, Jessie heard the shrieks of three little kids as they ran to their beloved cow's stall.

"Is she okay?" The oldest girl, who looked

to be about twelve, was leaning over the rails looking anxiously at the pair.

"She's just fine. But let's give her some time with her baby before you go in there, okay?"

"Okay."

The two other kids were peering through the slats; the youngest one had a blanket clamped close to his chest.

Jessie's throat tightened. She'd always thought she would have children by now. But vet school had been long and exhausting, and Jason just hadn't seemed interested in having a family. She'd convinced herself she didn't need it either. But now...?

What would it be like to have your biggest worry be about whether or not your kids would name a farm animal?

She shook the longing away and finished her job. The placenta emerged perfect and whole, and the baby was now on her feet, nursing with loud slurps that made her smile. She was strong, seeming no worse for wear after the ordeal her mom had gone through in getting her into this world.

"I don't know how we can thank you. I really appreciate your coming right out."

"It was no problem." She'd had to reschedule three of her appointments, but her clients had understood. She imagined Doc had had to do this more than once.

Her legs had finally stopped shaking, and Jessie could now draw a deep stress-relieving breath.

She smiled at the kids, cooing and laughing over the new baby, although they'd probably seen lot of animal births on this farm. But this cow was different. And this birth was special.

Like making love to Cabe had been? Was that why she'd been so desperate to put him in his place afterward. Because it had been special, when she didn't want it to be?

Maybe.

Which was probably why she'd been avoiding calling him to confirm that he was still coming on Saturday.

Surely he would have contacted her and let her know if he'd planned on backing out.

But it wasn't professional on her part. It wasn't what she'd done when preparing for Lillian's arrival. Because Cabe was special?

Oh, God. He was not special. He couldn't be. She did not need this right now.

But no matter how uncomfortable seeing him was going to be, she was going to call him and do the right thing when she got back to the office. Confirm he was coming. And maybe soften what had felt like a harsh ending to their encounter on Sunday. He'd been called to what might have been an emergency, and all she could do was rattle out words about nothing changing and blah, blah, blah…

How would she have felt if the roles had been reversed and she'd been called to help Jasmine, while Cabe was busy throwing the same words at her?

She wouldn't have appreciated it.

So she would do what she could now that she'd had time to realize the difference between what she'd done and what she *should* have done at the time.

She would apologize. And hope to hell he accepted it.

Margo had told him she'd been called away on an emergency and that she might be a while. But she said it was okay for him to wait, if he wanted to. Since the waiting room was empty, he did. He really didn't want to just show up on Saturday and hope for the best, even though his brain argued it would be the easier path. Easy wasn't necessarily the best path.

Rocky found her way over to him and yapped at his feet. He scooped her up, smiling as she licked his chin. "Are you still here, girl?" He glanced up at Margo. "No luck finding her owner?"

"Not yet. I almost think Jessie's hoping there won't be one."

The door to the clinic opened with the breezy sound of canned wind chimes— a holdover from Doc—and Jessie swept through. He blinked at the ponytail that was half falling out, some of her blond strands curling around her face. Her black jeans were covered in some kind of grayish dirt and her light blue shirt... Well, he didn't even want to think about what that large dark spot was on her left breast.

She headed toward Margo, who held up her hand for her to stop.

"What is it? Another emergency?"

"I have no idea. Look behind you."

Jessie's head turned in his direction and her eyes widened, lips parting. "Cabe..."

He stood, his glance going to Margo's face and seeing blatant curiosity there. He set Rocky on the ground. "Can I bend your ear for a minute? Outside?"

"Oh...of course." She glanced down at her clothes, her hand going up to shove back a loose hank of hair that draped over her shoulder. Rocky pawed at her leg until she picked her up. "Can you give me about ten minutes?"

"Sure."

As she went by, Margo said, "Your next appointment isn't for a couple of hours. I wasn't sure how long you'd be over at Jonas Tate's place."

"Good call. Thanks."

She disappeared into the back, leaving him alone in the waiting room. With Margo. Who had to be dying of curiosity. Well, this was one thing he was not about to discuss with anyone except for Jessie.

So he picked up the nearest magazine, so he didn't have to carry on a conversation with her, and flipped through it, reading nothing. But the very act helped keep him from thinking about all the things Jessie could say to him.

Like, "thanks but no thanks."

He took surreptitious glances at his watch in between page turns. Seven minutes went by and the door to the inner office opened once again, and Jessie emerged. Her hair was neatly in place, although it was wet as if she'd showered. And she was dressed in fresh clothes. If he hadn't seen her a moment earlier, he wouldn't have believed the quick transformation was possible. And when she came and stood over him, he could have sworn the scent of fresh honeysuckle followed her path.

"Care to get some coffee? From the coffee shop down the road?"

That last sentence was a little louder than the first one had been, and it was probably for the benefit of the receptionist, although her gaze never strayed there.

"Sure. Where did Rocky go?"

"She's in my office in a playpen."

That made him smile as he got up and held the door open for her. They left the clinic, but when he started to head toward his car, she shook her head, a half smile on her face. "Do you mind if I drive this time? That way I won't be stranded if you get a sudden call."

A reference to the precursor of their love-making, when she'd waited at the bottom of the Dome for him to finish his rescue. But she'd said she would have waited even if she'd had her own car. That and her smile said her words had been a joke.

But right now, it was hard to separate things that were funny from things that weren't so funny.

He waited for her to unlock her side of the door and climbed in. Suddenly the scent of honeysuckle was no more, and it was replaced by the smell of...

"Oh, God. Sorry. Maybe we should take your car after all so mine can air out."

That made him laugh. "Your emergency call was to an organic fertilizer factory?"

"Kind of. A cow in labor. She and I got up close and personal for a little while."

Kind of like he and Jessie had. Well, without the lingering aroma, he would hope.

So they got out, while Jessie opened all the windows on her car and headed over to Cabe's. His vehicle didn't have the same smell at the moment, but he was sure there were days when he was sweaty and the aroma was pretty rank. And his mom had always called cow manure the smell of fresh country air. He'd never really minded it.

He drove the few minutes to the Café Parisienne, although he couldn't imagine anything less like his mental image of Paris than the simple coffee and sandwich shop. He parked, but before he could open the door to get out, she asked. "Do they have takeout?"

"They do. I'll go in and get them. What do you want?"

"A cappuccino, extra whipped cream."

That made him smile. From cow poop to extra whipped cream. The woman was certainly a patchwork of contrasts. He found that he liked it. She could get down and dirty with the best of them. But she could also enjoy the frillier things of life. His ex had always chafed at how "small town" Santa Medina was. And when they'd divorced she'd made a bigger change than that. She moved away. The funny thing was, while she'd pressed him to start a family, she'd never pressured him to move away from their hometown. And really, of the two, he would have been more likely to give in to the second request than the first.

He got their orders and returned to the car, handing her her paper cup. "Here you go."

Climbing back into his seat, he set his drink on the cupholder, watching as she removed her lid and blew across her beverage for a few seconds before snapping the cover back on.

"Can we go out by the meadows?" she asked.

"Tuolumne?"

"Yes, if it's okay?"

"Not a problem."

He drove the fifteen minutes to the park area and showed his pass to get in. He then found one of the parking areas where they could look out over the water of the lake.

"Well," she said. "I know you wanted to bend my ear. But I'd actually planned to call you when I got back to the clinic today. I wanted to apologize for not getting in touch with you about Saturday's seminar and to say I hope you're still willing to come and present." She paused. "I also want to say I'm sorry for the way I handled…er, things on Sunday. You got a phone call which, for all I knew, could have been an emergency, and

I started blasting you with things that were of no importance."

"They were."

"What?"

He sighed. "They were of importance. You don't have to apologize. I actually came to apologize for much the same thing. Sunday was unexpected, and I can only chalk it up to the adrenaline generated by the rescue and…" he had to bite out the next words. "Emotional exhaustion. It felt good just to do something…normal."

Sunday had been anything but normal, but it was the only word he could think of to describe it without making things weirder than they already were between them.

"Normal." She laughed. "Okay, well that might have been 'normal' for you, but it was pretty extraordinary by my standards."

His brows went up, even as he fought to contain a laugh of his own. "I was talking in generalities. But as far as specifics go? Yes… pretty extraordinary."

"Not that it can happen again," she was quick to add. "Right before I moved to Santa Medina, I broke up with a longtime boyfriend. Let's just say the end wasn't pretty. So…"

"You're not in the market."

"Not at all."

A frisson of relief mixed with something else went through him. "I can well understand. I went through a messy divorce, myself, some years ago, so be glad your relationship never got to that point."

"Believe me, I'm thankful for that every day. Especially since he was stealing meds from me."

He turned to look at her. "Seriously?"

"Yep. Worse, he was taking a portion of the narcotics that were meant for my dog who had cancer. We were living together at the time and treating her with pain meds and chemo drugs to extend her time, but…" She took a deep breath. "He offered to treat her while I was at work. And now I understand why."

"How did you find out?"

"Her meds ran out quicker than they should have right about the time he'd weaned himself off pain meds after a shoulder injury—he's a minor league pitcher. There's more, but suffice it to say, now more than ever, I don't like secrets." She shrugged. "So, like you said, I am definitely not in the market anymore."

"I understand, truly I do. I know firsthand what it's like living with an addict." It was on the tip of his tongue to say more, but something held him back.

"Margo mentioned that you were divorced. You and your ex-wife were high school sweethearts, right?"

She'd jumped to the conclusion that the addict he'd been talking about was Jackie. While he might not want to talk about his dad, he also didn't want to let her believe something that wasn't true. "Yes, we were, but Jackie wasn't the one with the problem. It was my dad. He was an alcoholic."

She sat there for a minute without saying anything. "I didn't know."

He was surprised Margo hadn't told her. They'd all gone to the same high school together. Jackie and Margo were good friends, in fact. Margo didn't speak to him for a while after the divorce was finalized. It appeared time healed all wounds, since they were on speaking terms again.

Thoughts of his dad skittered through his

head. Well, maybe it didn't heal all wounds. Because the damage caused by his relationship with his dad had ultimately wrecked his ability to give Jackie what she'd needed. And if there was one thing about his marriage that he regretted the most, it was that.

"Jackie and I knew each other a long time, but once we got married she realized she didn't know as much about me as she thought she had." He cocked a shoulder in a half shrug. "So she left."

"I'm sure that was hard. I thought I knew Jason, but once we moved in together..." She winced, then smiled. "To top it all off, he couldn't stand Dumble."

Just like that, she popped the bubble of melancholy that had taken over the conversation. And he appreciated that more than she would ever know.

"Dumble? No! I can't even fathom how that would be possible."

"Are we talking about the same Dumble?" Jessie laughed again, and he found that he really liked the sound of it. Lilting and musical, the sound kind of melted into him every time he heard it. Which always made him tense. He didn't want anything sliding past the layers of armor he wore. Which meant he had to stay on his guard, because if he wasn't careful...

Well, he could find what he'd always been looking for, while foisting on her what he wouldn't wish on his worst enemy: him with all of his worn baggage and problems. Jackie hadn't been able to deal with it, why did he think someone else could?

Jessie took a sip of her coffee and leaned back against the seat, staring through the windshield. "Who knew places like this existed in the world? It's so calm. So serene."

"It is right now. But wait a few months. Yosemite can rage with the best of them. The roads up here close once late fall arrives."

"I hope I at least get to see the snow up here before that happens."

"It's beautiful in winter. Once the roads close, people visit it using cross-country skis."

"I see I'm going to have plenty of classes to take. Mountain climbing...skiing..."

"You've never skied?"

Her nose crinkled. "I've water-skied, but nothing involving snow."

It was on the tip of his tongue to offer her pointers on that too, but he didn't think they'd be well received. Especially since they were still trying to find their way through the aftermath of Sunday.

"Well, if you get the chance. Do it. There's nothing quite like it."

She took another long drink of her coffee. "I will. Thanks. So we're good on the other issue? And you're okay with coming on Saturday?"

"Yes." He frowned for a second. "Didn't you say you wanted to see the demonstration before that happened?"

"Well, I think I got as close to a real rescue as I want to get. No preview needed. I trust you guys to do what you do best. I'll just print up a pamphlet telling people it's at the Stately Pleasure Dome, and I'm sure they'll find it."

Well, that was pretty much it. He couldn't think of anything else that needed hashing out, and if she was okay with where things stood then he was too.

Except for that little part of him that had just raised its hand and asked to be heard.

Nope. Not happening. He ignored the request and gave Jessie a perfunctory smile, and they headed back to town.

CHAPTER EIGHT

CABE'S SECOND SEMINAR went as well as the first one had, and as Cabe stood at the front answering questions from the people who flocked around him, Jessie couldn't help watching him with admiration. Was there anything the man didn't do well?

He and Soldier had put on a first-class performance just like they had the previous week, and she'd learned things about Cabe that she hadn't known before.

Oh, she'd known he was in the army. But what she hadn't known was that he'd had a friend who had gotten lost in a deeply wooded area and hadn't been found until it was too late. That had sparked his desire to join a search and rescue team. And although she'd known that Solder was adopted from the shelter, she didn't know he'd been a natural and had taken to SAR training with gusto.

She'd also noticed that while he talked about his mom, he'd never mentioned his dad, which was understandable after what he'd shared with her. If she'd thought the ending with Jason had been bad, she couldn't even imagine living with an alcoholic for your whole childhood.

She waited until the crush of people became just one or two before she headed up to the front of the room. Soldier greeted her with a wagging tail, his droopy features at odds with that single happy-looking feature. It made her smile and reminded her so much of his owner. Cabe had many of the traits that Soldier possessed.

Bending down to pet him, she murmured, "Good job, buddy."

An old man stepped up to him. "Hey, your dad would have been proud. A shame that it ended the way it did."

In a flash, Cabe's demeanor changed. Oh, the smile was still there as big as ever, but his eyes had hardened to flint. It made Jessie want to shrink back. She'd seen Cabe laughing. She'd seen him intense. She'd seen him upset. And over the last week and a half they'd seemed to come back to where they'd started. But in all of her dealings with him, she'd never seen him like this.

Exactly how bad had his childhood been?

"Yes, you're right, it was a damned shame." And that one stilted sentence ended the conversation, the man turning to leave, as the one person left smiled at Cabe and gave a quick congratulations before she too turned and headed for the door.

Jessie took her hand off Soldier's head and waited for the door to close one last time before looking at him. "Are you okay?"

"Yeah. No. Hell, no one's mentioned my dad in a very long time. At least not to my face."

"I know he was an alcoholic, but you think he wouldn't have been proud of you? In some way, shape or form?"

He fixed her with that same hard steely look. "Oh, I don't just think. I know. He wasn't proud of anyone. Not even himself. He didn't just drink, he was a falling-down-until-someone-put-him-to-bed drunk. He was literally the definition of someone committing suicide by bottle."

Her heart went still. And she could see why he'd been so short with the older man. "I am so sorry. I can't imagine what that must have been like for you." She drew him over to one of the chairs and sat down with him. The clinic was closed since it was a Saturday, so no one was around, not even Margo, who was on one of her infamous fishing trips. "And your mom?"

"She finally divorced him when I was fourteen, after years of begging and pleading with him to stop drinking. And after a couple of black eyes that she explained away as accidents. He died of cirrhosis at the age of forty-two."

"God. Did he hit you too?"

"No. Only my mom."

Jessie swallowed. You would never know from being around Cabe that he'd grown up in an abusive household. But then again, lots of people kept dark secrets and covered them with a flashy smile. Just like Jason. Only it wasn't quite the same thing. In fact, when she'd first met Cabe she remembered thinking how much darker he was than Jason. She guessed she now knew the reason for that. Had that played into his divorce?

Not something she was going to ask him. So she said, "Is there anything I can do to help?"

He peered at her for a long moment. "I don't think so. After all this time, it is what it is. My relationship with my dad, or what little of it there was, is set in stone. There's nothing anyone can do to change it. Or him. It's too late."

"For him, maybe. But not for you. You've done well for yourself. Your dad might not have been proud of you, but you should be proud of yourself."

If anything, the tension in his face and jaw increased. "Easier said than done. As is not perpetuating any cycles that he set into motion."

Something about that made her shiver. Did he drink?

"And you're afraid you might perpetuate them how? Do you get falling-down-until-someone-puts-you-to-bed drunk?" She waited for a moment and then he shook his head. She gave an inward sigh of relief. "From what I can see you're a mature, caring individual who is in the business of rescuing people."

Something shot a bolt of lightning through her, making her sit up. "Was your friend the only reason you joined SAR?"

He gave her a hard smile. "I think you went into the wrong profession."

She was right, she sensed his dad was part of that equation. But he'd put her firmly in her place, and she knew better than to dig any deeper. But she couldn't blame him. It was really none of her business. But despite some of her earlier missteps with him, she cared about him. More than she probably should.

"I'm in exactly the right profession. Working with animals probably saves me a lot of grief."

"Oh, undoubtedly. Because, believe me, working with people is hard. Very hard." He smiled and stood up. "And now that you know the ugly, bitter truth about my childhood, can we promise we won't talk about this anymore?"

"Yes. I promise." She promised to not talk about a whole lot more than just his past. Or examine her current state of emotions, which were a jumbled mixture she wasn't sure how to sort through. Or if she even should. Part of that was probably wrapped up in how deeply he cared for Soldier.

Weren't people suckers for men with puppies?

Yep. She was starting to consider Cabe a friend—kind of, sort of—and she didn't want to do anything to mess that up. At least not any more than she already had. No more mining for information about him. She knew as much as she needed to know. As much as she wanted to know.

"Thanks," he said. "I appreciate that. And Doug, Brad and I ran through our mock rescue for next week and it went according to plan. It should take around thirty minutes at the most. Maybe less, depending on how tired I am that day."

The thought of how tired he'd been the time he'd rescued that woman came back to her. Did she, or anyone, really have a right to expect him to put on a show for the masses? "Cabe, if it's going to be too much, please don't think you have to go through with it."

"No, I want to. It's not just about the demonstration and letting people know about the SAR program. I think it's important for people to know how dangerous climbing can be.

Maybe they'll take more precautions. Put in the redundancies that we talked about a couple of weeks ago."

Kind of like she'd done in trying to keep from falling into a pool of emotions where he was concerned?

Well, like he'd said, maybe she needed to realize how dangerous it was to let herself get hung up on someone without knowing if they were a good match. Look how that had worked out with Jason.

"Yes, you said redundancies are always good. I did remember that much."

He smiled and this time his face softened. "Yes, you did. As long as you keep remembering that you shouldn't get into any trouble."

Ha! That showed how much he knew about her. Well, right now she was swimming as fast as she could away from the whirlpool that was her heart and hoping beyond hope that she could make it safely to shore before she was sucked under completely.

Demonstration day—or D-day, as Brad referred to it—had arrived. Cabe was more nervous than he normally was. Not because they would have an audience, but because any training practice had the potential to go sideways. And after Soldier had been hurt a month ago, he wondered if he should be taking chances with his dog's life like this. But Soldier was well trained for this, and he had to keep up that training or there was even more potential for him to be injured. It was like a redundancy that he'd talked about with Jessie.

Doug, Cabe and Soldier stood at the bottom of the Dome with about twenty people milling around, waiting for them to get started. It was almost one thirty and he'd seen no sign of Jessie yet, which surprised him. He'd spoken to her on the phone this morning and everything seemed to be in line. Then he saw her hurrying toward them.

"Sorry," she said. "There was a problem with Jasmine's calf, and I had to go."

His head tilted. "Jasmine?"

"Never mind, I'll tell you about it later." She greeted Doug and Terry—who'd come out to watch. "Thanks for coming and helping with this. Is Brad already up there somewhere?"

"Yep, he's there," Doug responded.

She glanced at her watch. "Are we ready?"

"Whenever you are."

"Okay, let me just get everyone gathered."

Cabe watched as she motioned for those who were here to watch to come closer, and she introduced everyone. "You guys already know Cabe and Soldier from the last two weeks. But this is Doug Trapper, one of the team members on the Santa Medina Search and Rescue team. Bradley Sentenna is our mock victim…you can meet him afterward. And then…" She glanced at her notes. "Terry Jordan…can you raise your hand so people can see you? There he is. He's the head of the search and rescue team here."

She looked around. "So I'm not going to give a lot of explanations, I just want you to see this fantastic team in action. If you have questions afterward about how to get involved, I'm sure any one of them can send you in the right direction." She smiled. "Okay, Cabe, handing it over to you."

Cabe nodded to her and then caught Doug's eye, silently asking if he was ready.

"Yep. Go."

Pulling the piece of Brad's shirt out of a notebook, he called Soldier closer and let him

sniff it. The dog lifted his head, probably rec-
ognizing Brad's scent right away. And then
he was off, scrambling up the hill, giving
a braying bark every time he found where
Brad had set his feet. They hadn't wanted
to make it too easy, so Brad had jumped
from one rock to another, trying to throw
Soldier off the scent. When his dog got to
that exact spot, he swept along a path that
any grid maker would be proud of and then
picked up the scent again. He took off with
sure feet, heading up the Dome. Ten minutes
later, the dog stood stock-still and barked and
barked. Brad stood up from his hiding place
and waved a piece of ripped cloth.

"Help! I need help!"

His voice carried down with enough re-
alism that a few people whispered among
themselves.

Cabe and Doug got to work, donning their
climbing harnesses and equipment as Brad
sank back into the bushes. Soldier might
have been able to make it up that slope, but
they'd chosen one that would require him
and Doug to using climbing gear.

They went through the whole process of
checking each other's gear, even though

they'd both done thousands of training climbs. It didn't matter how many you did. All it took was one mistake. One slipup to spell disaster for everyone involved. It was about keeping everyone safe.

"Belay?" he called over to Doug.

"Belay on."

"Climbing."

"Climb on."

Cabe started up the face of the rock and went until he found the first anchor bolt. He quickly hooked into it and then waited for Doug to follow him up. The procedure repeated until they reached Brad. They brought him out of the trees so people could see them pretending to check him over and treat him. And once done, they slowly helped their injured and lost climber head back down the Dome.

Once down, he glanced at his watch. Twenty-eight minutes. Not bad. Rewarding Soldier with a treat, Brad wiped the fake blood from his head to much applause.

Then, armed with the pamphlets Terry had printed up, they talked with people for the next half hour or so. There was a lot of general excitement about the program and those who couldn't or weren't able to go through a stringent training program still wanted to help. There were other options available, whether working in dispatch or even just raising awareness of the program.

He glanced up, his eyes seeking out Jessie before he realized what he was doing and then turned his attention back to the next person in line. He hadn't seen her, but surely she wouldn't have left until it was over.

Except she had. There was no real reason for her to stick around.

Maybe that calf she'd mentioned had taken another turn for the worse.

She'd talked about doing something for those involved in the mock rescue afterward as her way of saying thanks. She hadn't said what it was, though, just that it would take about an hour. They'd all said they could be there for whatever it was. Maybe it was some kind of reception at the clinic.

Then the people were gone, and Jessie reappeared as if by magic. Her smile was brilliant, and when she looked at him, there was this gleam…

There wasn't a gleam. It was his imagination.

"Hey, guys, can you follow me?"

He tilted his head. "Are we walking? Driving?"

"Walking."

Okay, that was weird. Where were they walking to? There were no restaurants up here, other than a local store that carried necessities for hikers or campers.

He looked at the other three members of the SAR team and Brad just shrugged. But they followed Jessie as she walked down the road, around the turn and then around another, sharper turn, and then Cabe saw them.

People. A whole slew of people. There had to be a hundred of them, at least. Music started as the Santa Medina marching band began playing, and as they got closer, four members of what he thought was the color guard, moved to the front of the gathering with some kind of rolled-up paper. And when they paired off, moving away from each other in a synchronized movement, the scroll unfurled. Across the enormous dark blue field appeared the words *We're so Proud of You!* in bold white letters.

Cabe stopped walking, and when his eyes somehow met Jessie's he knew...*knew* that

that message was for him. Was because of what she'd overheard in her clinic last week.

She came over and shook each of their hands and gave Soldier a treat.

He looked at her. "How did you...?"

"Actually, Margo did. I asked her to get the word out that we wanted to do something special for you...for the team and she hit it out of the ballpark. Everyone in town who was free today came out."

From out of the crowd stepped Doug's wife. Then Terry's grown children. Brad's sister and parents followed them. And he spotted Doc Humphrey, who gave him a gruff nod, out in the crowd as well. And suddenly, there was... Cabe's mom. They all came over and hugged their loved ones. As his mom wrapped her arms around his waist, bitter tears crawled up his throat looking for an exit. He held them in, hugging her tightly, and looked over her shoulder, realizing Jessie had slipped back into the crowd.

He didn't see Margo yet, but he'd bet she was out there somewhere.

But what he didn't understand was how one of the most talkative people in Santa Medina had managed to keep this a secret? Actually she hadn't. Maybe it hadn't been meant to be a secret from anyone but the team itself.

But it was one of the most special things anyone had ever done for their team. For him, personally.

And although Margo had been the mouthpiece, Jessie had initiated and orchestrated the gathering. Jessie…a kind and caring soul who would go to tend a sickly calf, just because someone called her and asked her to. One who adopted a lost and frightened dog that had been trapped on the dome. One who'd treated Soldier's wounds with gentle hands. The same hands that had patched Cabe back up.

Letting go of his mom and guiding her to stand beside him, he looked at her and said words he should have said many, many years ago. Words that out of his anger and bitterness he'd not been able to bring himself to say. "Thank you, Mom. For everything."

Her hand went to her mouth and tears shimmered in her eyes before she turned and buried her face in his chest, her shoulders trembling. When he glanced at the other members of Santa Medina's SAR, he saw similar scenes of tears and smiles and... gratefulness.

Terry had lost his wife six months ago, so this gathering had to be bittersweet for him, but he stood there in the embrace of his kids and looked like the luckiest guy on the face of the planet.

Cabe was beginning to realize just how lucky this town was to have the new veterinarian. Everyone had loved Doc and had sworn there'd never be another one like him, but he knew for a fact that there was. And it was Jessie.

He managed to catch sight of her once again and mouthed, "Thank you." He was pretty sure he was speaking for the whole town. And Jessie gave him a nod that said it all. She was happy to do it.

He leaned down to listen to something his mom said to him and when he looked up again, Jessie was nowhere to be seen.

She was probably in the crowd somewhere talking with people, because she was good at that. Such a great advocate for both animals and for the community as a whole.

Someone came over and handed him a

bag. "This is for Soldier. They're made specially for dogs by a shop in Mariposa. When Jessie told us about this two weeks ago, we found a store that makes them from scratch. I hope he likes them."

"Thank you." He took a small steak-shaped treat from the bag and handed it to Soldier, who gobbled it up. He laughed. "I think he approves."

By the time things ran their course and he'd stopped by the refreshment table with his mom, the floral tablecloth blowing in the breeze, it was starting to thin out. Margo was manning the refreshments. He gave her a grin. "You're a sneaky one, Margo."

"What can I say? You guys deserve it. But it was really Jessie's idea."

"Well, thank you." He'd said the words so many times, he wondered if they'd be etched on his tombstone. He glanced around again for Jessie but didn't see her. "Speaking of Jessie, is she still here?"

"No, she left about a half hour ago. Not sure why. Maybe she had a patient."

"Yes, maybe she did."

But for some reason, he didn't think so.

He waited around and saw his mother off, promising to set up a time for lunch with her soon. It had been ages since he had, and it was long overdue. Jessie's reception had helped him see to that.

He thought she'd probably helped him with a whole lot of things without either of them realizing it.

Well, she was probably exhausted, so first thing tomorrow, he would run over to the clinic and give her a proper thank-you for everything she'd done for the community. For him.

If anyone had deserved this party, it was her. With her new ideas and new enthusiasm, she could very well breathe some new life into a town that had sat steeped in tradition for far too long.

Her reach had even extended into the station house, where Terry had agreed to take on Carrie, the shelter dog. Already she was ensconced on a leopard-print pillow fit for a queen. And he was pretty sure the rows of kibble that lined their pantry shelves was proof that she was already well loved by the men who spent so much time at the station.

Yep, Jessie had reached into hearts throughout Santa Medina. She wasn't Doc. But maybe she was exactly what this town needed—what *he* needed—at this moment in time.

CHAPTER NINE

JESSIE HADN'T BEEN able to stay yesterday. The scene between Cabe and his mom had been too raw. Too painful. Especially knowing what she did about his father. The weight of it had been etched on Cabe's face, and she'd wondered if she'd made a terrible mistake in opening the reception up to the general public. She hadn't really thought about his mom when she'd asked Margo to organize things. Hadn't even realized she still lived in town. But she was glad so many members of the community had shown up in support.

Then she saw Cabe say something to his mom. Watched as the woman turned and sobbed into the paramedic's chest. Watched as he looked up over his mother's shoulder and mouthed "thank you" at her. She'd turned away in tears.

The gathering hadn't been the wrong thing.

But something else might very well be. Because what she'd thought—hoped—might be a temporary clog of emotions concreted itself into something that could not be brushed away or hidden. And as she stood there, she was suddenly terrified that he was going to read the truth on her face. And there was no changing it. No denying it. She loved the man.

Despite the terrible truths she'd learned from her last relationship. Despite learning a deep painful truth about Cabe. Or maybe that was part of it. She'd done exactly what she was afraid of doing and had fallen head over heels for him. And it horrified her. She had no idea what to do about it, except to bury it deep and hide it. From him. From Margo. From the world.

As she sat in her empty clinic on Sunday morning, she tried to figure out what to do about it.

Maybe he felt the same way. But she didn't think so. It wasn't like she could just walk up to him and ask him. Because if he didn't…

She would be devastated. Would want to run. Because her fight-or-flight instinct had always been firmly rooted in flight. After all, she'd fled San Francisco right after learning about Jason's addiction, and although it had been the right thing to do, she'd still taken the easy route and left town.

And found Santa Medina. A place she was coming to love deeply. Almost as much as she loved Cabe. Did she really want to walk away from everything she was building here—her career, her new practice, her new friends—if it turned out that Cabe didn't care about her in that way?

Maybe now was the time to learn a new way of dealing with conflict. The question was, could she do it?

Sleep had been a long time coming last night, although she'd texted Margo this morning to thank her for everything, including cleaning up afterwards.

Her phone made a pinging sound. She glanced down at it.

You're welcome, Jess. Oh, and by the way, Cabe was looking for you after you left. I told him you probs had a patient who needed you.

She had. Only the patient had been her. She'd needed to take some time for herself to think about what she was going to do, now that she'd found herself in a situation that could become very awkward for everyone. She wrote Margo back, avoiding the elephant in the room.

Thanks for covering for me.

Her phone pinged again.

No probs.

Margo cracked her up with her abbreviations, but it was on par with her rather eccentric nature.

Just as she put her phone away and started to vacate the chair Margo normally sat in, the chimes went off over her front door. Looking up, she saw it was... Cabe.

She was horrified.

Not only by what she'd been thinking about, but her gardening clothes and her messy hair. She honestly hadn't expected anyone to stop by.

"I thought I might find you here. Or Dumble did. He was yelling 'Get back here' over and over when I rang the bell."

"Oh, God." Despite the feelings of melancholy that had overwhelmed her for the past twelve hours she could still find humor in her bird. "He hates it when I leave. I guess if I ever have a break-in though, it might come in handy."

"It might." He took a couple of steps closer. "I wanted to come by and say thank you for yesterday."

She just stopped herself from parroting Margo's response, complete with the abbreviation for *no problem*. "That wasn't just me, it was everyone. We're all grateful for the work you do."

"And I'm grateful for what you do. This town is incredibly fortunate to have you."

"The town." Her heart sank lower.

"Yes. Several people have mentioned it, even Doc Humphrey. Did you know he was there?"

"I did. He was the one person I specifically invited. He wants to meet with me tomorrow afternoon to see how things have been going." She pulled in a deep breath. "Santa Medina is a special place."

"Yes, it is."

"Being here has been…well, I'm the one who feels fortunate."

He took a few more steps. "Do you?"

Looking into his eyes and trying to see anything there that might give her hope, she nodded. "I do."

His fingers touched hers and a bolt of emotion spiraled through her. She was so confused. So very mixed up about her place here in the town. Her place with him.

But one thing she did know. If this was going to end badly, she was going to make sure it ended spectacularly. On her terms. She was going to make sure he knew exactly how she felt about him. And then it was up to him. But maybe there was more than one way to show someone what they meant to you.

Her fingers curled around his. "Like I said… I feel very, very fortunate." She drew the words out slowly, infusing them with as much seduction as she knew how.

He looked as confused as she felt…for about half a second. Then, using her grip on his hand, he tugged her toward him, so fast that it knocked the wind out of her for a second.

"Jessie, do you have any idea what you..."

The rest of his words were lost as his lips came down on hers. God! Was that an admission? A prayer? An oath?

Right now, she didn't care, because hope—which had been looking for the tiniest of crumbs to devour—evidently found the fuel it needed and went drag racing through her veins, tires spinning, gravel flying.

And then there was no stopping this. And she didn't want to, even if she could.

She kissed him as if there were no tomorrow. Because for them, there might not be.

"Your place?" He lifted his head to look at her.

"No. Here."

His brows went up. "Are you expecting anyone to walk through that door?"

"No. No one's coming."

He smiled. "In that case..." Taking her with him to the door, he engaged the dead bolt and pulled the front blinds.

Then putting his hands on her hips, he walked her back toward him, sending her pulse soaring. Her hips hit his and what he wanted was very, very evident. That was good. Because she wanted it too.

Suddenly they were in the private exam room, and they couldn't get each other's clothes off fast enough. He leaned in and bit her lip. "Remember that mechanism that you promised could hold me?"

Breathless with need, all she could do was nod.

With a quick movement, the hands on her hips lifted her onto the exam table. He planted his palms on the table on either side of her thighs and leaned in to kiss her. "Which way is down."

It took her a second before she realized what he meant. Then, her breath in her throat, she murmured, "Left pedal."

He must have found it, because the table began its slow descent. Then it stopped. "That looks just about right."

"Right for—Oh!"

He hauled her to the very edge of the table, her legs spreading to accommodate his hips, and then it was all too clear what he was thinking. Because nestled between the V of her thighs was a very eager looking body part.

And then Cabe kissed her in earnest, and she took him. Took everything he had to give and hoped she could give back even more. She wanted to lay out all of her hopes and dreams on this table and prayed those offerings were enough for him. Enough to build a future on...together.

"Where is it?"

"Excuse me?" He leaned back to look at her with horrified eyes.

"No, not that. *That*, I can find. With both hands tied behind my back. Want to try?"

"Don't." Groaning, he pressed his forehead to hers. "You drive me crazy...do you know that?"

She hoped so. Hoped she drove him crazy enough to think this thing between them might just work. Might be something real. Something to cherish.

Smiling up at him, she said, "In that case, the thing I'm looking for starts with a *c* and ends with an *m*."

"Oh...*that* that."

"Yes, *that* that."

He opened his palm, like some kind of awesome magician, and there appeared a square wrapper, its cellophane top already ripped open.

"How did you... Never mind."

She took it from him, and this time, she did the sheathing, drawing the act out for as long as she could stand, her fingers trailing over each inch of naked skin as she rolled it down him.

He felt alive in her palm, reacting to each touch, each squeeze, each change in pressure.

"Enough, Jess. God. Enough." He trembled against her, pushing her hand away. "I need time to get you ready, to—"

"No. I've been ready ever since you got here." With that, she leaned back, supporting herself on the narrow table with her elbows. "Come see."

With that, he took himself in hand and found her. Slid home with a loud groan that echoed through the tiled room.

Her eyes shut as she relished each tug and thrust that brought her nerve endings to spectacular life. That made butterflies take flight behind her closed lids. Fluttering wings that surged higher with each new movement. Taking him deeper. Harder.

The wings coalesced until she could no longer tell one from the other, a beautiful kaleidoscope of color that pulled together, getting tighter and tighter until...

They exploded apart, taking her with them as surge after surge of pleasure poured over her…through her. Cabe wrapped his arms around her hips and drove hard and fast, groaning again as he found his own release.

They stayed there for several minutes, the sound of their breathing loud in the room.

Her eyelids slowly parted to find him staring at her with a weird expression. No one said anything for a second or two, then he broke the silence. "Hell. That was…that was…"

"I—I think I love you." The words stumbled out before she could stop them. They hung there like orphans hoping to find a place where they were wanted.

Oh, God, that was not how this was supposed to go. She'd wanted to ease into it. Feel him out a little more before taking that polar plunge. But now that she was all the way in, she could feel her skin turning frigid, her muscles cramping with fear.

"What?"

The single word hit her with staccato force, paralyzing her. But not him evidently, because he slid away from her with a fluid motion that made her want to weep. How easy it was for him to just pull…free.

What hope had dined on was evidently not enough to keep it going, because its engine sputtered and then died. And all that was left was Cabe, staring at her with this inscrutable expression.

She sat up in a rush. Well, she'd done it. Exactly what she'd said she was going to do. She gave a choked laugh. And she ended it just like she'd said she was going to. Spectacularly. With no ambiguity. No lingering questions.

"I think you should leave, Cabe."

He dragged a hand through his hair. "I can't… Hell, Jess, I can't give you what you need. What you deserve. Let me explain why—"

"No. No explanations needed. You've made it very plain. And it's made my decision easier." She pulled in a deep breath. The fact that he'd shortened her name and made an endearment out of it—all the while dropping a guillotine—just made everything that had happened here that much worse.

"Please. Leave."

See? She could throw staccato phrases right back at him.

Without another word, he gathered his clothes, but he didn't put them on in front of her. Instead, he turned and walked out of the room. Her last sight before he shut the door behind him, was his spectacular ass. The ass that was walking away from her for the very last time.

"Doc Humphrey is back..."
    "She's only been here two months, but..."
    "Think it might be a man? Of all things..."
    "She saved our calf."

He'd come to the diner to get a quick cup of coffee, four days after leaving Jessie's clinic, and was surrounded by snatches of conversation. He'd only been half listening until that last phrase came through loud and clear: "She saved our calf."

It could only mean they were talking about Jessie. He put all of the phrases together and came up with...

Jessie was leaving town?

Why?

Dammit, did he have to ask? It was pretty obvious. It was because of how they'd left things. No. Not "they." It was because of how *he'd* left things. He'd all but fallen head-first over his tongue in his effort to find the right words after she dropped that bombshell about love. To let her down easy.

Because, in the end, it didn't matter how he *felt*. Feelings were transient fickle things. He'd seen that firsthand. And if Cabe's life experiences had taught him anything, it was that he did not have what it took. To be a good husband. To be a good father. It didn't matter how he felt. Unless he could *do*, the feelings meant nothing.

So he'd had two choices, when Jess had told him she loved him. He could either hurt her now. Or he could hurt her later. Because there was no getting around it. He *would* hurt her.

By not knowing how to talk through his feelings.

By holding back emotionally because he was afraid of being rejected.

By pretending he *had* no emotions during the times when they were the most important thing. Just like he'd done when Jessie had told him she loved him. Just like he'd done with Jackie during their marriage.

All his father had *done* was display his emotions. Every damn emotion he'd ever had. And most of those had been bad. Had been hurtful. Every time Cabe had a negative emotional reaction to something, a little voice inside his head had whispered, "See? Just like the Daddy-o."

He could go through the laundry list of reasons he'd racked up about being wary of emotional attachments. Every year that list got a little bit longer until he was convinced he didn't need anything but Soldier and his work.

And then along came a sexy veterinarian that had him doubting himself all over again. She made him want to try. Made him want to fight.

But was his motive to add to her life? Or suck the life away from her?

And that's why he'd stood there with nothing to say. Because in truth, what could he say in the flaming aftermath of sex? Fantastic sex that had obliterated his expectations for all time. Nothing. Because he had no idea if that quavery little voice in his head was the sex talking. Or if they were from those elusive emotions that had become tangled around her from day one.

But if she's leaving.

Wasn't that her choice?

If so, she was going to make this awfully easy on him. And impossibly hard.

Maybe the best thing he could do for himself, for both of them…was to sit at home in the dark and do some heavy lifting in the emotional department and see if he could move some furniture around. Maybe, he'd find where he'd hidden his damned feelings.

Maybe then, they'd finally tell him what he needed to know: Go after her? Or just let her go?

CHAPTER TEN

Doc Humphrey stood there glaring at her. "What did you do to my damn files?"

"I digitized them. It makes it easier."

His gaze softened for a second. "I suppose I should be thanking you, rather than grumbling."

"I'm glad to have you back, Doc. Even if it's only for a day or two a week. Are you sure you don't want more?"

"No. Retirement isn't for me. Not right yet. But neither is taking over the clinic again. My tremors are better, thanks to some new-fangled meds. But it's just a matter of time. And I might like puttering in that garden you set up out front."

She shook her head with a smile. "We agreed the house was yours. But the garden is mine."

Jessie was doing her best to hold true to staying the course. With some help from friends, she'd moved Dumble, Rocky and her few possessions into the small apartment over the garage and let Doc move back into the house he'd lived in most of his adult life.

So far it was working out well. At least the apartment was.

She wasn't as sure about the whole "not running" thing. What she did know was she couldn't do her thinking in that house, where every day brought a reminder of what they'd done in that bed. It was going to be hard enough facing the memories from the clinic. Of witnessing those impossibly blue eyes shuttering themselves against her.

Maybe she'd decide that moving back to San Francisco was the right thing to do. But right now, when her wounds were too raw, too impossibly painful, she didn't trust herself to make any major changes.

The man surveyed her, then dropped into the chair next to hers, his voice suddenly soft. "How's it been going? Really? I've been around a long, long time. I saw those glances you and Cabe gave to each other at the gathering."

"Gathering?"

"What the town did for the SAR team."

"Oh." What else could she say? She could lie. But somehow it didn't seem right. And Doc was eventually going to realize she was avoiding Cabe. She'd already decided to ask him to take over Soldier's care and any exams. Although he'd already told her he'd feel better not having to do any surgeries.

"Things have changed, though, haven't they?" His hand covered hers. "Surely he wasn't that hard on you, girl." The gruffness in his voice belied the deep concern she heard just below the surface. It would have been worse if he'd come at her with accusations and disappointment.

"No. He wasn't. Everyone in the town has been wonderful." So many conversations came back to her. Delivering that calf for Farmer Jonas and his fear of his kids naming the baby. Patching up Soldier and watching the townsfolk rally around the SAR team. Hearing Cabe's heartbreaking confession about his father. Was that what some of this was about? His dad?

It didn't matter. If he was so damaged that

he didn't have the capacity to love her, then she wasn't going to settle for anything less. No matter how much she enjoyed his company. No matter how much his lovemaking meant to her. Some people might not need the words, but she did. She'd had them her whole life from her parents…from her extended family.

And she deserved them. Just as much as Cabe deserved hearing them from whomever he was involved with.

"I love this town, Doc. It's just that…" How easy it was to think of him that way. Because of the impact the town had made on her.

"Do you love something besides this town?" He gave a sigh and patted her hand. "You won't find a man better than Cabe."

"I know. He…he just said he can't give me what I need." She avoided mentioning her ill-timed confession of love.

He puffed out his cheeks. "What is it you need, Jessica Ann Swinton?"

She stared at him for several seconds. "Jessie isn't actually short for Jessica, and Ann isn't my—"

"I know all that, but it's what I would have named you if you'd been my daughter."

She laughed to keep him from seeing how touched she was by his words, by the meaning behind them. But really, did the man actually know how impossible he was?

His wily eyes said he did, and he just didn't care.

Why couldn't she be more like him? With less care and a more "live and let live but do it my way" attitude.

She could see why people loved this man. He snuck up on them while they weren't paying attention and...*boom*! You loved him.

Wasn't that exactly what had happened with Cabe. He'd snuck up on her while she wasn't looking...and she fell in love.

"So you haven't answered my question. What is it you want?"

Looking into Doc's rheumy eyes and grizzled face, she said, "I want Cabe. But I want all of him. Not just the part he's willing to let me have."

So what was she going to do about it? The old Jessie would have run and not looked back. But the Jessie she *wanted* to be was telling her to stay...but to really examine her reasons for doing so and consider the ramifications, if it turned out that Cabe really didn't want love. And then, only then, could she be at peace with her decision.

And maybe she'd give Cabe some space to think without the pressure of her constant presence. Maybe he couldn't care less if she stayed or went. But the thought that he might, made her feel better.

She curled her fingers around Doc's and squeezed. "Would you mind if I took a few days off? If there's an emergency, I'll be right upstairs. I just need some time to think."

"Go ahead and think, girl. But give yourself permission to go after what you want. Even if what you want turns out to be not quite right for you in the long run. Like my trial run with retirement."

"Thanks, Doc."

They both stood up, and she was shocked when the man caught her in a bear hug that she thought might squeeze the life out of her. Then he released her and headed over to where his rusted file drawers used to be. "So where the hell did you put the actual files, anyway?"

On that note, she went through the door

and closed it behind her. She wished she could catch the town in the same bear hug that Doc had just given her. But she couldn't. But she was going to try to love them every bit as hard as Doc had. Every bit as hard as she loved Cabe.

Then she headed up the stairs to her little apartment, which held most of her earthly possessions, including Dumble and Rocky, the pup they'd rescued from the Dome. The bird gave her a sideways look the second she opened the door. "Not the only one."

"Not the only one, what, Dumble? I have no idea what that even means."

The bird looked at her. "Not the only one." He gave a loud squawk as soon as the words were out.

Jessie laughed at his response until she could laugh no more. Until her laughter turned to silent tears that crept down her cheeks and seeped into the lonely areas of her heart.

Cabe avoided the diner for the next two days. The last thing he wanted or needed right now was to hear the latest gossip about Jessie.

Because he was pretty sure he'd heard all he needed to hear. That she was thinking of leaving because of some man.

It was pretty obvious who that man was. So what did he do? Confront her and tell her not to be stupid. That this town needed her and that she shouldn't take off because of one foolish idiot who'd failed to keep it in his pants.

The crass phrase made him cringe. Because whether he admitted it out loud or not, the sex *had* meant something. It had meant too much, actually. He hadn't guarded himself like he normally did, and she'd slid in below his radar.

Even Soldier noticed the change in him since Jessie's confession. And unlike him, his dog mirrored back his moods better than those silly fortune-teller rings they used to sell. Or maybe they still did. He was pretty sure his ring would have an easy time of it. It would show black. All the damn time.

But was he willing to let her leave town over someone like him? Maybe he could go and tell her something like, "Well, if I could feel anything for anybody, I would have picked you."

And if that wasn't some kind of morose greeting card message, he didn't know what was.

So why not go over with no plan in mind and tell her why he had done and said what he had. Which had pretty much been nothing. Oh, he'd tried, but Jessie had been too hurt to listen at the time. But maybe now that a couple days had gone by, she'd be more receptive. And maybe this time, he could actually come up with some better words.

Fortified by that, he decided to pay her a call. In person. Before it was too late. And since it was Sunday afternoon, she was pretty sure to be home, right?

So he made the short drive over, surprised when her little blue car wasn't in her parking space. Instead, there was a gray sedan that looked fairly new. Maybe she'd bought a new vehicle.

They hadn't actually said when she was leaving, but he'd assumed it wouldn't be until she'd found another vet to take her place. What if he was wrong?

At the door he hesitated. What if some stranger's face met his? What if Jessie's smile never greeted him again?

Realizing he'd forgotten to draw a breath, he sucked down a couple of gulps of air, feeling suddenly lost. Feeling suddenly afraid to see what was on the other side of that door.

But whether he was afraid or not, it would change nothing.

So he knocked. Waited. Knocked again. Louder this time.

After a few more minutes, he thought he heard shuffling from inside.

"Jessie?"

The door flew open. "Dammit it, Cabe. I was in the middle of the best dream I ever had. I was in the...well, on some island somewhere. And it was a place I could actually get some sleep!"

"Doc? What are you doing here?"

"Nice to see you too, Cabe. Thanks for the warm welcome back."

"Back, as in...?"

"Yep, I'm working at the clinic again."

The news made him reel backward as if he'd been struck by lightning. He'd thought he had more time. After all, it had taken Doc a while to find Jessie. "You're back full-time?"

"Would that be so unbelievable?" He

stepped back. "Get in here before I decide that visiting my dream island is preferable to standing here gabbing with you."

Cabe moved into the space. It looked exactly the same as when Jessie had lived here. But then again, that was because she hadn't gotten around to changing out Doc's decor. He guessed that made it nice for Doc to come back to.

"Sit, and I'll get you some coffee. The pot is still on."

"No thanks, I'm good." Doc's coffee was thick and black, and the most unappetizing brew he'd ever tasted.

"So if you don't want coffee or chitchat, what are you here for?"

Yeah, what was he here for? He had no idea. But he certainly wasn't going to tell Doc any of that.

Doc took a closer look at him, then this godawful smirk appeared on his face. "You expected to find Jessica here instead of me, didn't you?"

"Jessica?" He faltered for a minute. Was the man worse than he'd been before? "Do you mean Jessie?"

"Of course I mean her. Who else would I mean?"

He couched his next words in the vaguest terms he could think of. "Did Jessie move?"

"Yes, she moved. Didn't she tell anyone besides me?" The smirk vanished as suddenly as it'd appeared.

"I've been busy for the last day or so, so maybe she did. I…just wasn't aware she was leaving."

The man's eyes narrowed. "Oh, I think you knew *something* was going to hit the fan, didn't you?"

Okay, so he hadn't failed memory-wise in the short time he'd been away. He was as sharp as ever. Cabe glanced at the man's hands for a long moment.

"Steadier than you expected? The big city doc had some concoction that slowed down my shakes. At least for now."

Which explained why Doc was back at the clinic. But that still left the question of where Jessie was.

"I'm really glad, Doc. Was it your idea to take the clinic back over?"

"Let's just say it was a mutual decision."

"Hell, Doc, let's stop dancing around the subject. Is Jessie gone for good or not."

"Pretty sure that's something you should be asking her yourself."

Yes, it was. And if she had already left Santa Medina?

What had he expected? That even though he didn't want to take the cake out of the baker's window and share his life with it, that it would somehow magically just stay there for his viewing pleasure? That he could go and stare longingly at it whenever he wanted to? Imagine the taste of it on his tongue? What it would be like to call it his?

That's kind of exactly what he'd thought.

Until that option was no longer there. Until the threat of never seeing that cake again loomed on the horizon. Never was a very, very long time.

That word made an area of his heart hurt in a way he hadn't felt for a very long while. The spot spread its tentacles out until they wrapped around the entire organ, squeezing it tighter and tighter.

Mourning her.

Because he loved her.

But what if love wasn't enough. It hadn't

been enough for his mom who had given and given and given to a man who'd given nothing in return.

But would Cabe truly let that happen? Would he let Jessie waste her life on him? Or was he willing to stand up and fight to give her what she needed. No matter how hard it was. No matter how alien it might feel to do so.

It didn't feel alien with Soldier, did it?

No. It didn't.

He took a deep breath and looked Doc in the eye. "I take it she's gone back to San Francisco."

"Not quite."

The prevarication made him laugh.

"Come on, Doc. If you get me an address, maybe I can get you back to your nice cushy retirement spot."

"I'm kind of liking where I am, to tell you the truth." He gave a dramatic pause. "I would get you an actual address, but I can't remember it and they got rid of my file drawers. And right now Margo's—"

"Gone fishing." He finished Doc's sentence for him.

"Yep. Some things around this town never change."

Maybe. But Cabe was about to see if some things could change. For the better. Namely...himself.

"I guess I'll have to try to find her myself."

Doc laughed. "I didn't say I didn't know where she was. I just said I couldn't remember the address. She's right upstairs. In the apartment over my garage."

CHAPTER ELEVEN

JESSIE TRIED TO sit in her new place and do some thinking, like she'd promised Doc she'd do, but it was harder than she expected. She felt lonely and so out of sorts that she didn't know which end was up. For the thousandth time, she wondered if she should just go back to her parents' house in San Francisco. But she had a feeling those old sayings about never being able to go home again held an element of truth. It had been almost a week since she and Cabe had made love in that clinic, and she'd heard nothing from him. Not that she'd expected to.

And she was no closer to making a decision about him. Although Dumble had.

He recited "Not the only one" constantly now, and she was pretty sure it had something to do with Cabe. Maybe he'd made the odd comment and Dumble had picked up on some emotion behind the phrase.

She'd video chatted with her mom yesterday and, between gasped sobs and with a voice that was almost too hoarse to speak, she'd somehow gotten her story out. Oh, not about the sex parts, but about the rest. About how she'd fallen in love with Cabe, and that he was the most wonderful man, but with a terrible dad who had somehow robbed his son of the ability to be happy.

"Get this. He never told his son he was proud of him. Not one single time."

By the time she was done, her mom was crying along with her.

"I love him, Mom, but I just don't know what to do."

Dumble threw his two cents' worth in from beside her. "Not the only one!"

"Probably not, buddy. But it sure feels that way."

"What is your heart telling you to do, Jess?"

Over the last three weeks, she'd gained some important perspective. She missed Cabe so much she could barely breathe.

Could she really face him again? God. She just didn't know.

"It's telling me not to give up. Even when I probably should."

Her mom dabbed at her eyes with a tissue. "Maybe that's the very time you shouldn't. When you should just hold on a little while longer."

"You always did see the best in every situation."

"Maybe because I got my happy-ever-after, and he's a pretty good one. It sounds like Cabe is as well. So make very sure, before you make any permanent decisions. We would love to have you back home, so don't take this the wrong way, but I feel like Santa Medina is where you belong. No matter what Cabe decides."

Maybe that's why she'd felt so weird whenever she thought about running back to San Fran.

"I think you're right. And, you know what? I think I can handle it."

Her mom leaned closer to the screen. "I absolutely know you can."

"I love you so much. And I'm so glad you guys are my parents."

Her mom blew her a kiss and Jessie pretended to catch it in her hand. "I'll call you if anything changes."

"I'll be right here. Cheering you on, no matter what."

With that they ended the call. Her dad had already left for work hours ago, but she already knew he would support her decision too. She went outside and sank on the little bench in her garden and tugged at a weed here and there. Doc was in the office today and had given her an update. He seemed happy to be back at work. Well...as happy as his gruff manner would allow him to be.

But he'd probably be glad to know she was going to stick around Santa Medina.

No matter what Cabe decided, it wouldn't change her decision. She loved him. Would love him for a very long time. But she would make her life in the town that she also loved.

Sliding from the bench and getting down on her knees, she began to weed the garden in earnest, so caught up in the task that she almost missed the shadow that fell over her.

Until she heard her name.

"Jess?"

She looked up, shielding her eyes against

the glare of the sun. Then her breath left her body in a huge whoosh.

Realizing she was just sitting there staring at him, she lifted her chin a fraction. "Cabe? What are you doing here?"

"I could say that I'm Doc's errand boy, but would you believe that?"

"No."

"How about the fact that the whole town is mad at me, and they believe you're leaving Santa Medina because of me."

"They would be wrong about me leaving. But if I did leave, they'd be right about the reasons." To soften the words, she allowed the merest hint of a smile to cross her lips.

"Would you mind standing up, you're making me uncomfortable down there."

"There are enough weeds for two." She smiled again. "Down here."

"Weeds."

"It seems some of us have more than others."

He knelt beside her and at once she was transported back to a month ago, when she'd reveled in his touch, in the scent of his skin. She closed her eyes against the memories for a minute.

He didn't say anything, just went about the task of pulling stuff up.

She touched his hand. "Uh-uh. That's a flower."

"How can you tell the difference?"

He stared at the plants, most of which were still in their early stages. She understood his confusion.

"You eventually learn which ones should stay and which ones should go. But it takes time and experience."

He took her chin and tilted it, so she looked up at him. "Like emotions."

The fact that he caught what she was aiming for surprised her. "Yes. Exactly like that."

He sighed. "When you told me you loved me, I was shocked. The fact that you could know it with such certainty...amazed me. Scared me." He looked into her eyes. "You'll never know how much it scared me."

She pulled up another weed to avoid looking at him. "I think I do. Because I was just as scared. But I couldn't..." She tried to find the words. "I couldn't bear to go through life wondering what might have happened if I hadn't said the words. I didn't want the regret of not knowing." She gave a slight shrug. "And now that I do, well…"

"Except you don't." His jaw worked, a muscle twitching as if he fought something inside him that was probably telling him to hold it in. To not let whatever it was out. "I feel it too."

The words hung between them and hope surged. But it wasn't enough. Not at this point in her life. Not after all the heartache she'd suffered at someone else's hands.

"Feel what?" This was so important. So very important. She couldn't let him sit on the side of the pool and dip his toes in whenever he wanted to. She needed to hear the words. If he couldn't get past this…

Please, Cabe. Just say it.

If he could sacrifice in this area, he could sacrifice in others. Just like she would sacrifice for him.

"I love you." He closed his eyes and then opened them again, the blue irises seeming to be infused with a light that hadn't been there before. "I do. I have all along. I just felt it wasn't enough. The words…they mean nothing, if I can't give you what you need."

"Cabe." Tears prickled behind her eyes as she hugged him close. "You just did. You gave me exactly what I needed."

"But if I can't say *rah-rah-rah* every time you want me to, or—"

"Have I ever asked you to do that? I'm not a super *rah-rah-rah* person, if you haven't noticed."

"I don't always talk things out."

She took his chin between her thumb and forefinger and wiggled it back and forth. "You don't think I talk enough for the both of us?"

"Well…"

"Be careful with that answer, buddy."

He laughed, seeming to relax all at once.

She got serious. "I don't know what you think I want from you, but I think it's a whole lot less than you think it is. I want companionship, can you give me that?"

He nodded.

"I want to periodically hear the words. Not all the time. But sometimes."

He nodded again. "I can do that."

"I want children, can you give me that?"

"I want to, but…"

There was a long pause that made her hold her breath. Then something in his face changed. Got softer, his glance going to her midsection in a way that made her swallow.

A huge feeling of relief made her want to laugh, but she held it back. She didn't know why, but she sensed he'd kicked down some mental barrier and had come out on the other side. She forced herself to remain matter-of-fact and keep things light.

"But nothing." She looked closer. "Unless you have a problem with sperm count."

He looked shocked, and this time she did laugh. "Okay, I take it those guys are pretty good swimmers."

"As far as I know." His brows went up. "You can find out for yourself later."

He waited as if expecting her to come up with some more conditions.

She smiled. "That's it, Cabe. I'm now ready for your expectations."

"Mine?" He swallowed. "Okay. I would ask for your patience as I learn to tell—"

he motioned to the garden "—flowers from weeds."

"That's easy."

"I would like honesty."

She sensed that one came from a place deep inside of him. A place of hurt and sadness. And she wanted to weep for him. But that's not what he'd asked for. So she held it inside her.

"I'll give you honesty."

"And I want to make you proud."

This time she couldn't hold back the tears. "Oh, Cabe, you've had that since the time I watched you rescue Gloria from that mountain. I love you. And I'm very, very proud of you. More than you'll ever know."

He pulled her against him and held her there for a very long time. This time he smiled. "It looks like we've come to a working agreement."

"I think we have, indeed, Mr. McBride."

He kissed her, then looked at her. "Why didn't you tell me your real name is Jessica?"

She laughed. "It's not. And that could have only come from Doc."

"Yes, it did. And he seems rather put out by his missing file cabinet." He stood and held out his hand for her. She took it, and he pulled her to her feet.

"Oh, wait! I have one more demand," she said.

The expression on his face made her laugh. "No, it's nothing terrible. I should have said it's a request, not a demand."

"What is it?"

"Is there any way you could…um, rip a pair of your jeans right along here…" she traced her fingers down his right buttock, "and periodically walk around the house in them?"

His choked laughter told her she'd hit the right button. In more ways than one.

"I think that can be arranged." He glanced toward the garage. "So you're living there right now?"

"Yes I am."

He gave her a smile that she could only describe as calculating. "Does there happen to be anyone else up there right now?"

"Just Dumble and Rocky, but they probably don't count."

"Dumble might. It depends. He tends to be a tattletale."

"Yes, he does. He also knows how to parrot certain, possibly embarrassing, sounds."

His lips pursed. "That could be a problem. How loud exactly are you planning to be?"

The hope that had died a hard death, was back on top…making its triumphal lap around the track.

"I can be as loud as you want me to be." She thought for a second. "Well, I'd rather the whole clinic not hear us."

"I can agree with that."

She led him up the stairs and into the apartment. Rocky ran over to meet both of them, doing a dance on her hind feet. He scooped her up. "Well, hello there. Still no owner?"

"I think her new owner is going to be me."

The second he set the dog down and Dumble saw him, the bird bobbed his head up and down, his comb raising high on his head. "Not the only one! Not the only one!"

The words were pitched so high, they were almost a scream.

"Weird. Ever since we moved into the apartment, he's been repeating that constantly. Do you know where he got it from?"

"I do, but that's a long story. And I think

it can wait a while." He took her in his arms and kissed her as Dumble swiveled between making smooching sounds and loud screeches, and Rocky whined at their feet. "A very long while, if those two—and I— have our way."

CHAPTER TWELVE

SHE FINALLY GOT her wish to see Tuolumne in the snow. How fitting that it was on the first anniversary of their marriage. And it didn't disappoint. It was gorgeous with snow sweeping across the meadow and clinging to their Dome—as she had come to think of the Stately Pleasure Dome. It had brought her pleasure, in so many ways.

Her skis pulled to a halt so she could take it in. Her cheeks were on fire and her hat was askew, but she didn't care. The temperatures today were well below that of her disastrous polar plunge, when she'd blurted out that she was in love with him, while he was still trying to process his feelings. Still trying to process whether he was capable of being a good husband. A good father.

But process them he had. His seeking her

out had proven more than anything, that he *did* have what it took to give her what she needed. Because really? Her needs weren't all that great:

She wanted to be loved. By Cabe.

She wanted to have babies. By Cabe.

She wanted to prove that he was everything he needed to be and more. Because he was Cabe McBride.

And he. Was. Enough.

His father's tragic life and death had scarred him in ways that no one could truly understand. But she trusted him to keep remodeling himself into the person *he* could trust. Because she suspected he hadn't trusted himself in a very long time. Maybe even never. But he was learning to.

His arms slid beneath hers, coming to wrap around her midsection. "Are you sure the doctor said this was okay?"

"Hey, I pulled a calf yesterday, I think a little skiing isn't going to do either of us any harm."

By "us" she didn't mean her and Cabe. She meant her and Cabe and the little one she was carrying inside her. It was just a little peanut, too small for others to notice just yet, and she wanted to keep it that way for a little while longer. To be the secret that only she and Cabe knew about. Because each second he was with her, was another second he could prove to himself that he truly *was* the man she saw when she looked at him. They both had some growing and changing to do. But they were helping each other do exactly that.

"Did I tell you that Mom and Dad are actually thinking about moving to Santa Medina?"

He nuzzled her ear. "Why is that surprising? We have the best vet in the whole country."

"I think you might be a little biased."

"Speaking of biased. Did I tell you I saw Farmer Jonas yesterday in town?"

"No. How is he?"

Cabe chuckled. "He said to tell you, and I quote: 'They named that damn little heifer.' He didn't seem too happy about it, but said you'd know what he meant."

She spun around in his arms and said the words she'd repeated to him time and time again. "See? We *are* magic. When we're together, good things happen."

"So, naming 'that damn little heifer' is a good thing?"

"Yes. It's a very good thing. Because it means she's going to grow up and retire out in that pasture with her mother and live a long and happy life."

"Ah, yes, I can see how that is a very good thing." He kissed her lips, slowly deepening the contact until she was breathless with need. Then he pulled back. "I think you're the one who's magic. So when I retire, will you let me share your pasture with you?"

"I have a feeling we'll both have to be very old and very gray before that happens."

He straightened her hat. "I can feel myself graying as we speak. Which reminds me, we'd better head back before someone sends SAR out to find us."

"Yes, because we all know how that will go. They'll find us long before we want to be found. Especially with Soldier on the trail."

Cabe had made his peace with Dumble and could be found padding through the kitchen before dinner with the bird perched on his shoulder. Dumble had unfortunately picked up a few more choice sayings which Jessie was going to have to talk to him about.

Not Dumble, but Cabe who thought it was hilarious to teach her bird urban slang that wasn't fit for work. And Soldier and Rocky got along famously. It was as if they were made to be a family.

As they turned to go, Jessie threw one last look at her surroundings. "I am the luckiest girl on Tuolumne Meadows."

"Sweetheart, you're probably the *only* girl silly enough to be out on Tuolumne right now."

She gave him a secretive smile. "That doesn't make me any less lucky, does it?"

"No, it doesn't. So, then, am I the luckiest man out here?"

She gave him a hard peck on the lips. "Yes, you are. And I'll show you just how lucky when I get you home."

Without any urging whatsoever, Cabe began retracing their path across the snow, that fine ass of his moving faster than she'd ever seen it go. Well, maybe not faster...

Suddenly her skis picked up speed as well. And yes. She was the absolute luckiest girl in all of Tuolumne.

* * * * *